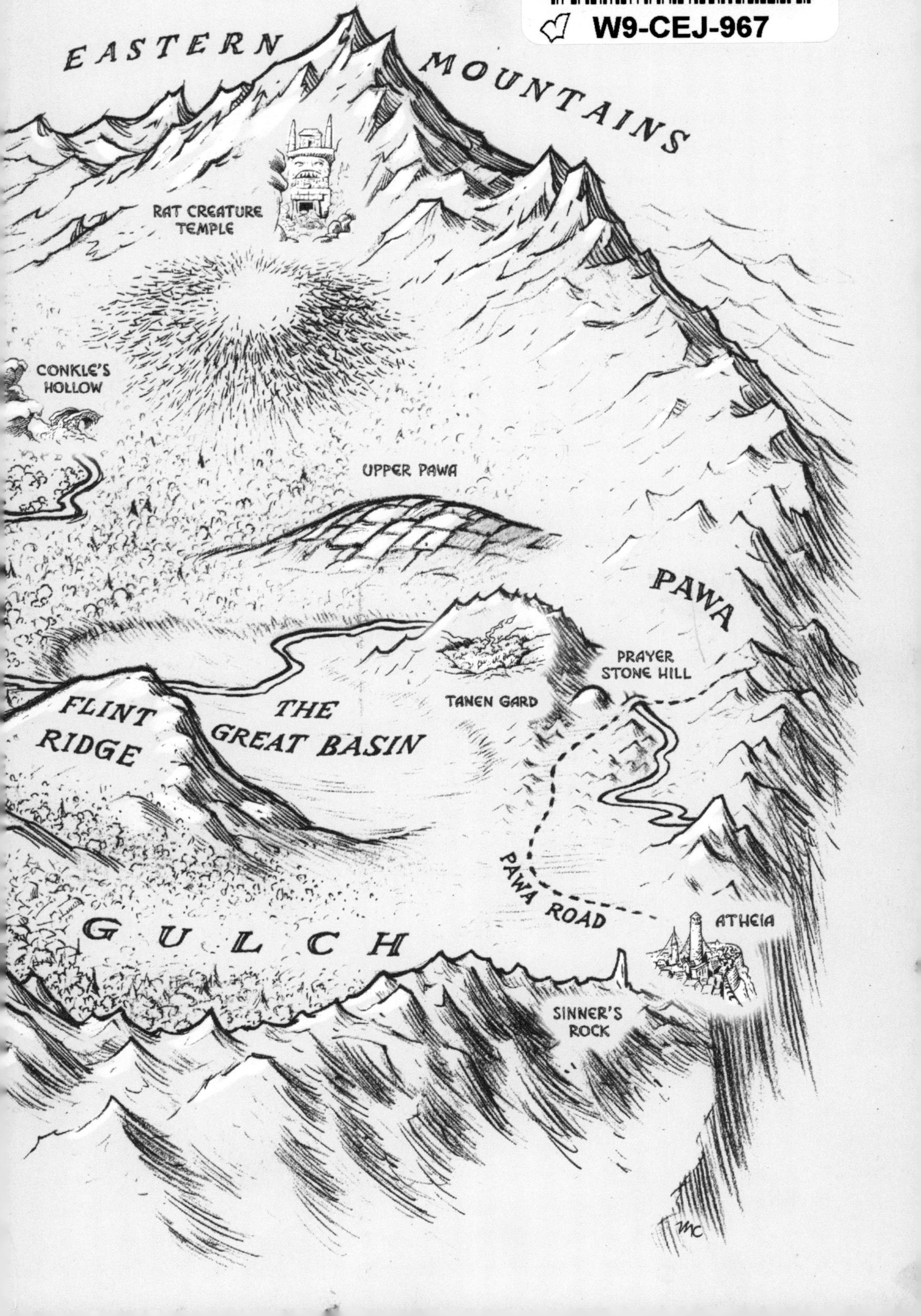
EASTERN MOUNTAINS
RAT CREATURE TEMPLE
CONKLE'S HOLLOW
UPPER PAWA
PAWA
PRAYER STONE HILL
TANEN GARD
FLINT RIDGE
THE GREAT BASIN
PAWA ROAD
ATHEIA
GULCH
SINNER'S ROCK
MC

Dreaming of Harvestar

ACCLAIM FOR JEFF SMITH'S

Named an all-time top ten graphic novel by **Time** *magazine.*

"As sweeping as the 'Lord of the Rings' cycle, but much funnier." —**Andrew Arnold, Time.com**

★*"This is first-class kid lit: exciting, funny, scary, and resonant enough that it will stick with readers for a long time."* —**Publishers Weekly,** *starred review*

PRAISE FOR *ROSE*

*"***ROSE** *is a magnificent prequel to Jeff Smith's* **BONE.**" —*Neil Gaiman, author of* **Coraline**

"I love Charles Vess' art so much that I'll buy anything he illustrates, but his collaboration with Jeff Smith on **ROSE** *has really upped the ante."* —*Charles de Lint, award-winning fantasy writer*

THE ***BONE*** SAGA

Out from Boneville

The Great Cow Race

Eyes of the Storm

The Dragonslayer

Rock Jaw: Master of the Eastern Border

Old Man's Cave

Ghost Circles

Treasure Hunters

Crown of Horns

ROSE

BY JEFF SMITH

WITH ILLUSTRATIONS BY CHARLES VESS

An Imprint of

■SCHOLASTIC

New York   Toronto   London   Auckland   Sydney   Mexico City   New Delhi   Hong Kong   Buenos Aires

This book is dedicated to Karen and Vijaya

Copyright © 2009 by Jeff Smith.

The chapters in this book were originally published in the comic book *ROSE* and are copyright © 2000, 2001, and 2002 by Jeff Smith. ROSE™ is © 2009 by Jeff Smith.

Library of Congress Catalog Card Number 9568403.

ISBN-13 978-0-545-13542-9 — ISBN-10 0-545-13542-7

ISBN 0-545-13543-5 (paperback)

ACKNOWLEDGMENTS

Harvestar Family Crest designed by Charles Vess

Map of *The Valley* by Mark Crilley

Illustration and font design by Charles Vess

10 9 8 7 6 5 4 3 2 1   09 10 11 12

First Scholastic edition, August 2009

Book design by David Saylor

Printed in Singapore 46

CONTENTS

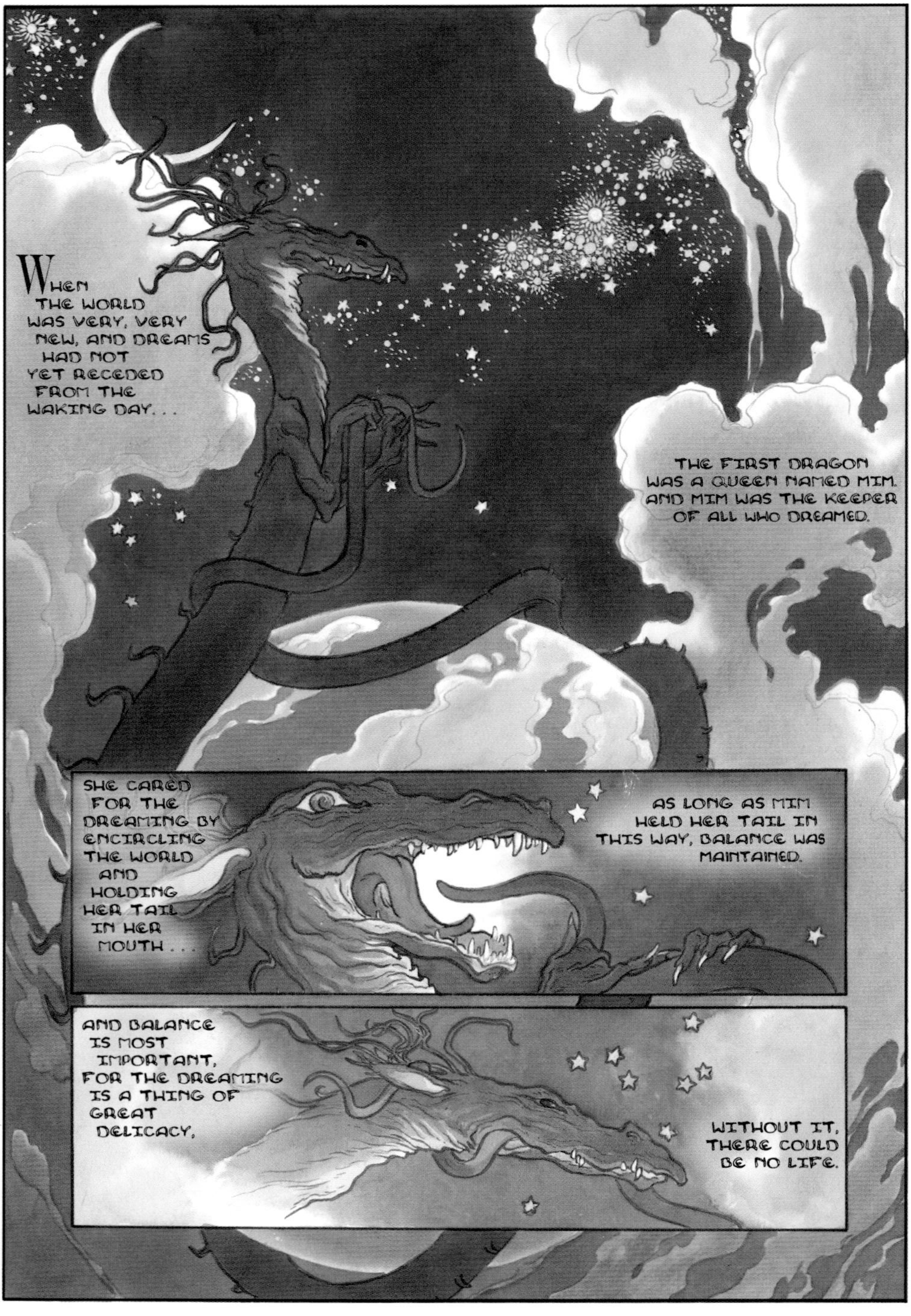
WHEN THE WORLD WAS VERY, VERY NEW, AND DREAMS HAD NOT YET RECEDED FROM THE WAKING DAY. . .
THE FIRST DRAGON WAS A QUEEN NAMED MIM. AND MIM WAS THE KEEPER OF ALL WHO DREAMED.
SHE CARED FOR THE DREAMING BY ENCIRCLING THE WORLD AND HOLDING HER TAIL IN HER MOUTH . . .
AS LONG AS MIM HELD HER TAIL IN THIS WAY, BALANCE WAS MAINTAINED.
AND BALANCE IS MOST IMPORTANT, FOR THE DREAMING IS A THING OF GREAT DELICACY,
WITHOUT IT, THERE COULD BE NO LIFE.

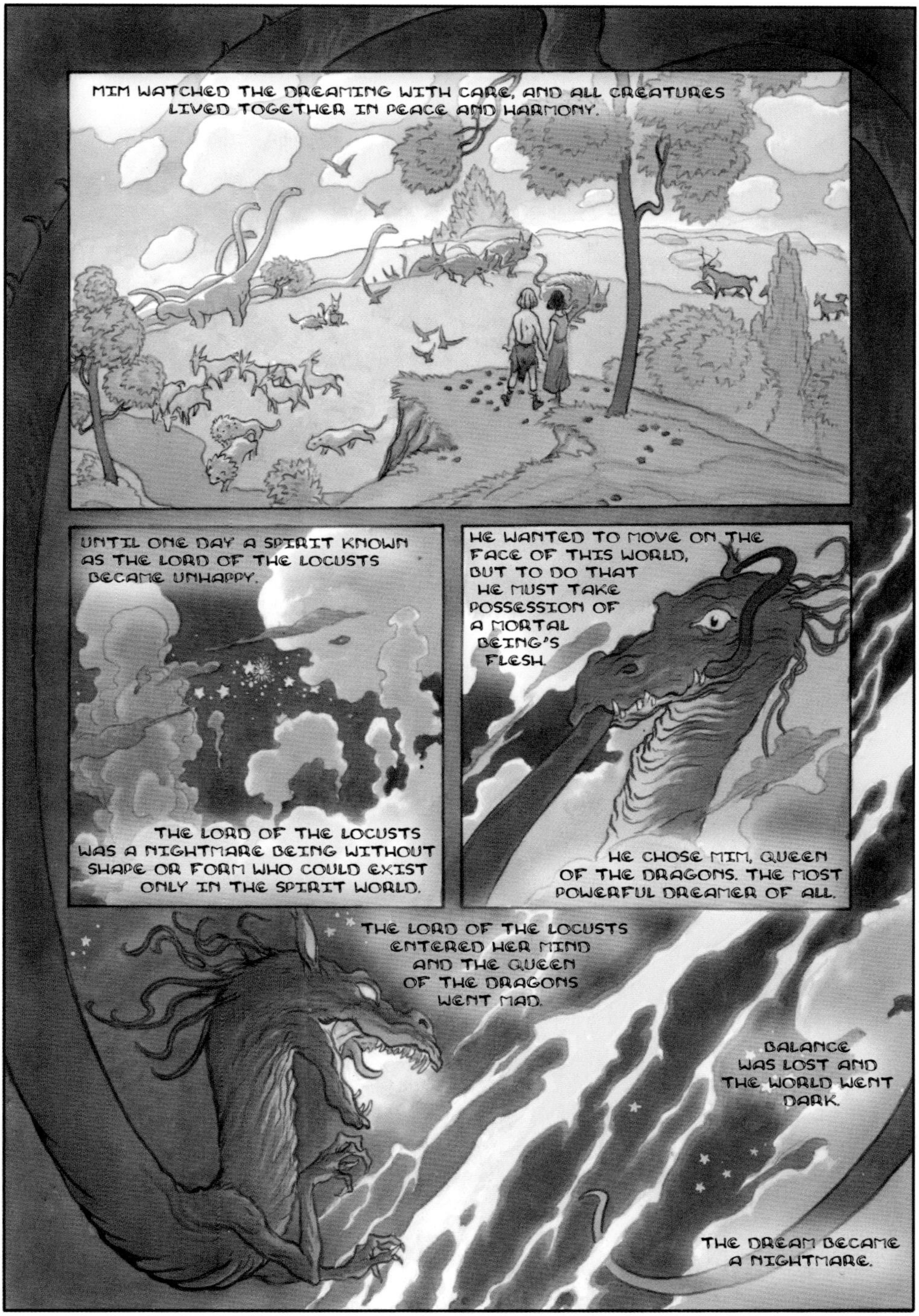
MIM WATCHED THE DREAMING WITH CARE, AND ALL CREATURES LIVED TOGETHER IN PEACE AND HARMONY.
UNTIL ONE DAY A SPIRIT KNOWN AS THE LORD OF THE LOCUSTS BECAME UNHAPPY.
THE LORD OF THE LOCUSTS WAS A NIGHTMARE BEING WITHOUT SHAPE OR FORM WHO COULD EXIST ONLY IN THE SPIRIT WORLD.
HE WANTED TO MOVE ON THE FACE OF THIS WORLD, BUT TO DO THAT HE MUST TAKE POSSESSION OF A MORTAL BEING'S FLESH.
HE CHOSE MIM, QUEEN OF THE DRAGONS. THE MOST POWERFUL DREAMER OF ALL.
THE LORD OF THE LOCUSTS ENTERED HER MIND AND THE QUEEN OF THE DRAGONS WENT MAD.
BALANCE WAS LOST AND THE WORLD WENT DARK.
THE DREAM BECAME A NIGHTMARE.

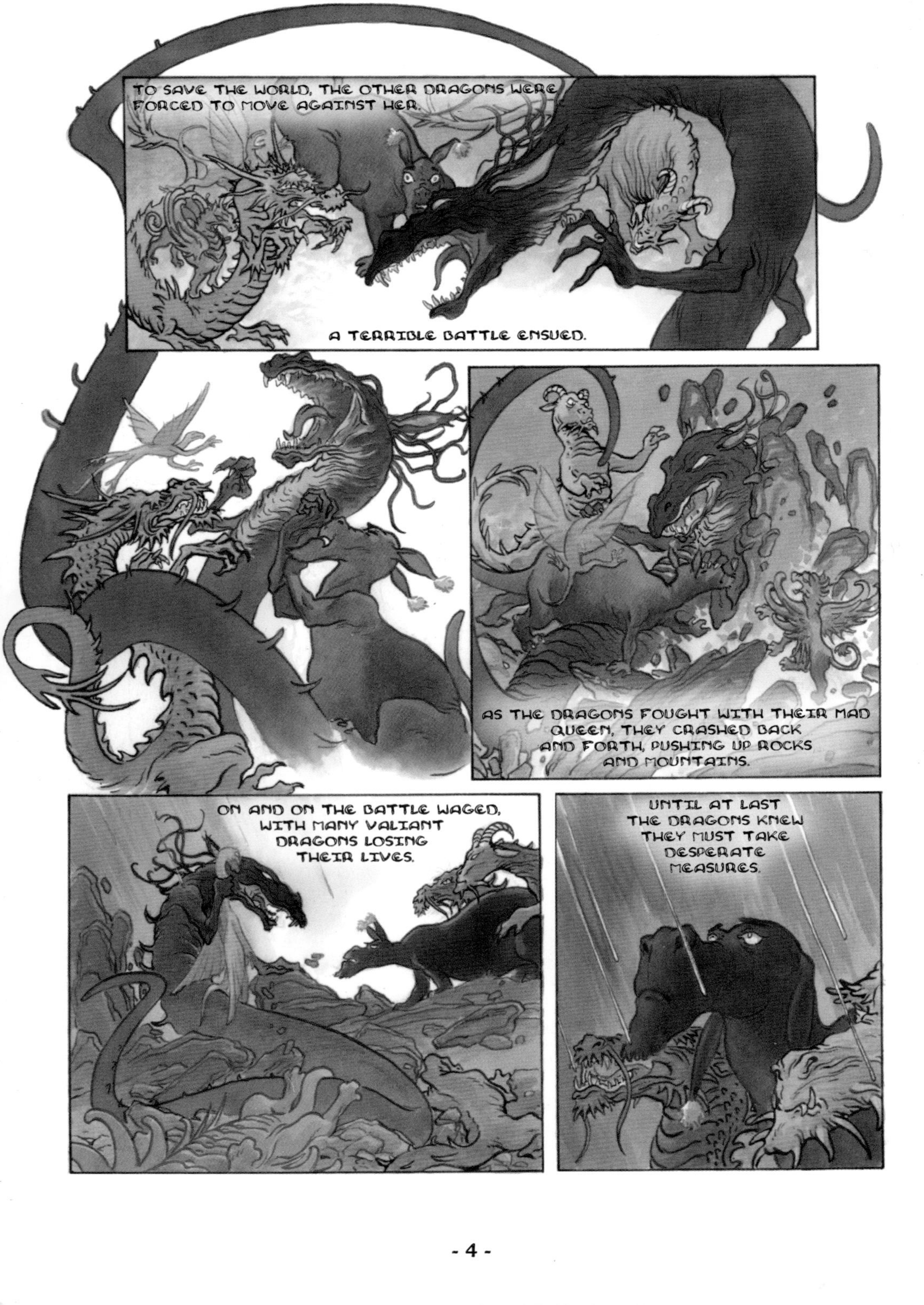
TO SAVE THE WORLD, THE OTHER DRAGONS WERE FORCED TO MOVE AGAINST HER.
A TERRIBLE BATTLE ENSUED.
AS THE DRAGONS FOUGHT WITH THEIR MAD QUEEN, THEY CRASHED BACK AND FORTH, PUSHING UP ROCKS AND MOUNTAINS.
ON AND ON THE BATTLE WAGED, WITH MANY VALIANT DRAGONS LOSING THEIR LIVES.
UNTIL AT LAST THE DRAGONS KNEW THEY MUST TAKE DESPERATE MEASURES.

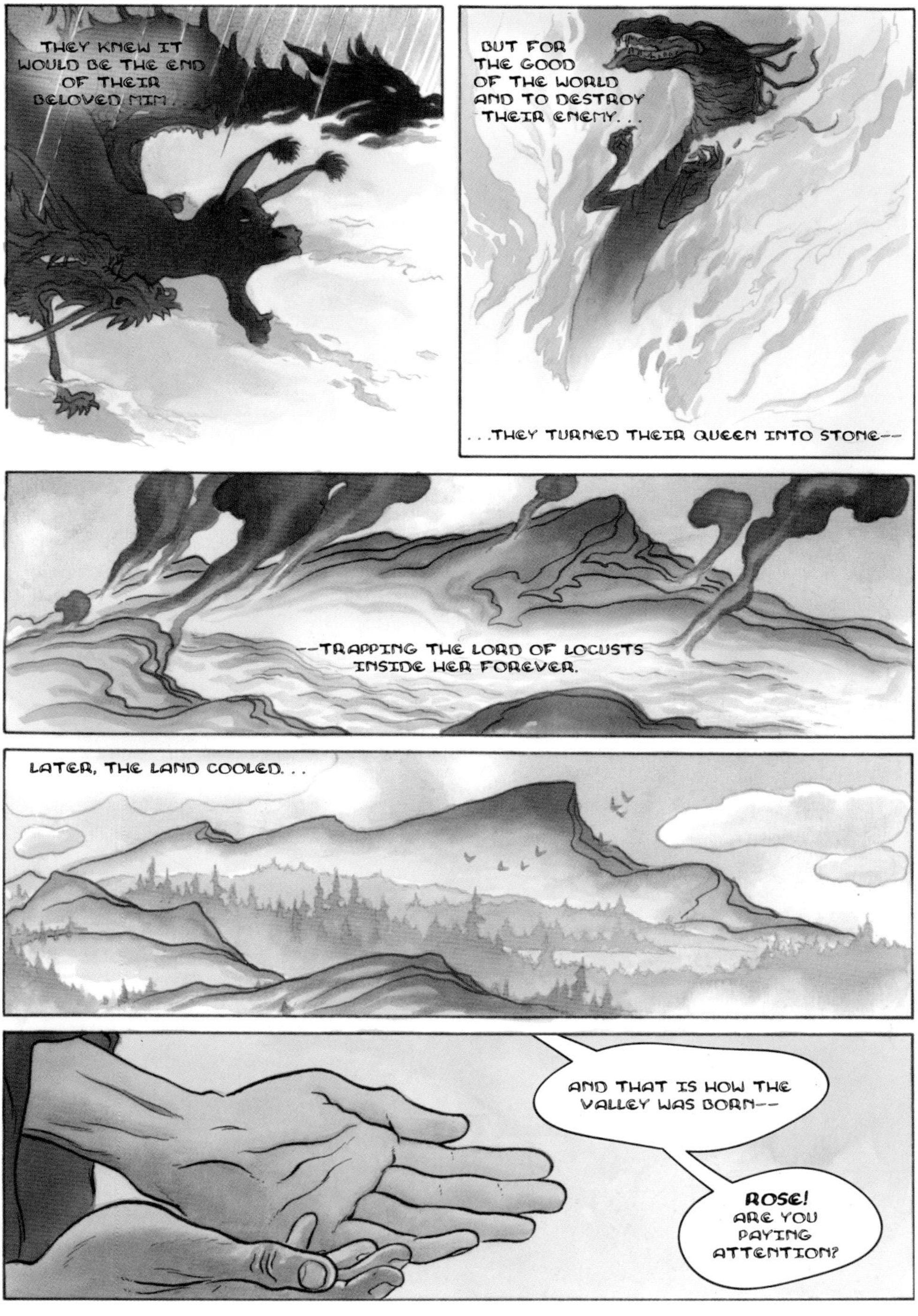
THEY KNEW IT WOULD BE THE END OF THEIR BELOVED MIM . . .
BUT FOR THE GOOD OF THE WORLD AND TO DESTROY THEIR ENEMY. . .
. . .THEY TURNED THEIR QUEEN INTO STONE--
--TRAPPING THE LORD OF LOCUSTS INSIDE HER FOREVER.
LATER, THE LAND COOLED. . .
AND THAT IS HOW THE VALLEY WAS BORN--
ROSE! ARE YOU PAYING ATTENTION?

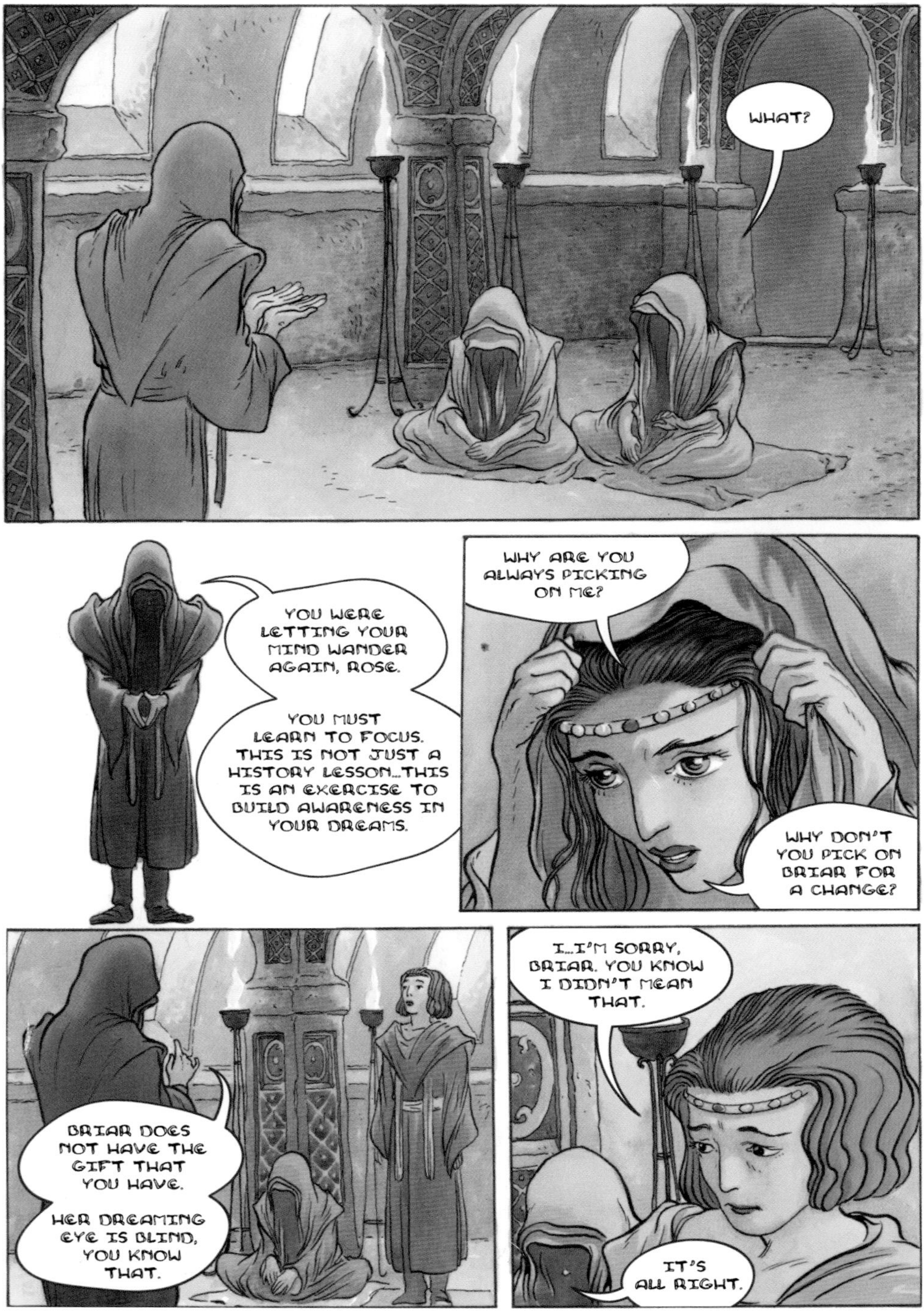
WHAT?
YOU WERE LETTING YOUR MIND WANDER AGAIN, ROSE.
YOU MUST LEARN TO FOCUS. THIS IS NOT JUST A HISTORY LESSON...THIS IS AN EXERCISE TO BUILD AWARENESS IN YOUR DREAMS.
WHY ARE YOU ALWAYS PICKING ON ME?
WHY DON'T YOU PICK ON BRIAR FOR A CHANGE?
BRIAR DOES NOT HAVE THE GIFT THAT YOU HAVE.
HER DREAMING EYE IS BLIND, YOU KNOW THAT.
I...I'M SORRY, BRIAR. YOU KNOW I DIDN'T MEAN THAT.
IT'S ALL RIGHT.

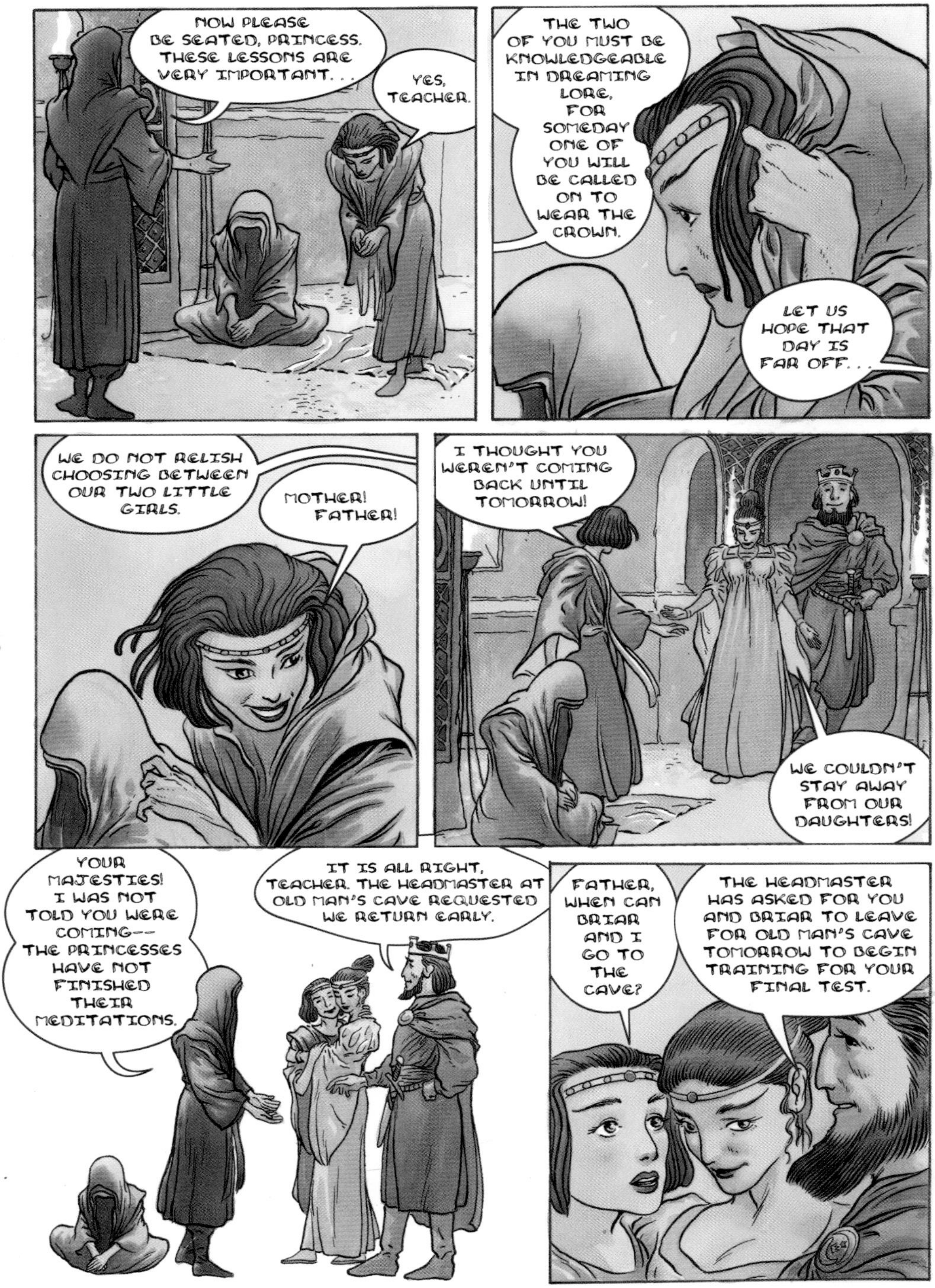
NOW PLEASE BE SEATED, PRINCESS. THESE LESSONS ARE VERY IMPORTANT. . .
YES, TEACHER.
THE TWO OF YOU MUST BE KNOWLEDGEABLE IN DREAMING LORE, FOR SOMEDAY ONE OF YOU WILL BE CALLED ON TO WEAR THE CROWN.
LET US HOPE THAT DAY IS FAR OFF. . .
WE DO NOT RELISH CHOOSING BETWEEN OUR TWO LITTLE GIRLS.
MOTHER! FATHER!
I THOUGHT YOU WEREN'T COMING BACK UNTIL TOMORROW!
WE COULDN'T STAY AWAY FROM OUR DAUGHTERS!
YOUR MAJESTIES! I WAS NOT TOLD YOU WERE COMING-- THE PRINCESSES HAVE NOT FINISHED THEIR MEDITATIONS.
IT IS ALL RIGHT, TEACHER. THE HEADMASTER AT OLD MAN'S CAVE REQUESTED WE RETURN EARLY.
FATHER, WHEN CAN BRIAR AND I GO TO THE CAVE?
THE HEADMASTER HAS ASKED FOR YOU AND BRIAR TO LEAVE FOR OLD MAN'S CAVE TOMORROW TO BEGIN TRAINING FOR YOUR FINAL TEST.

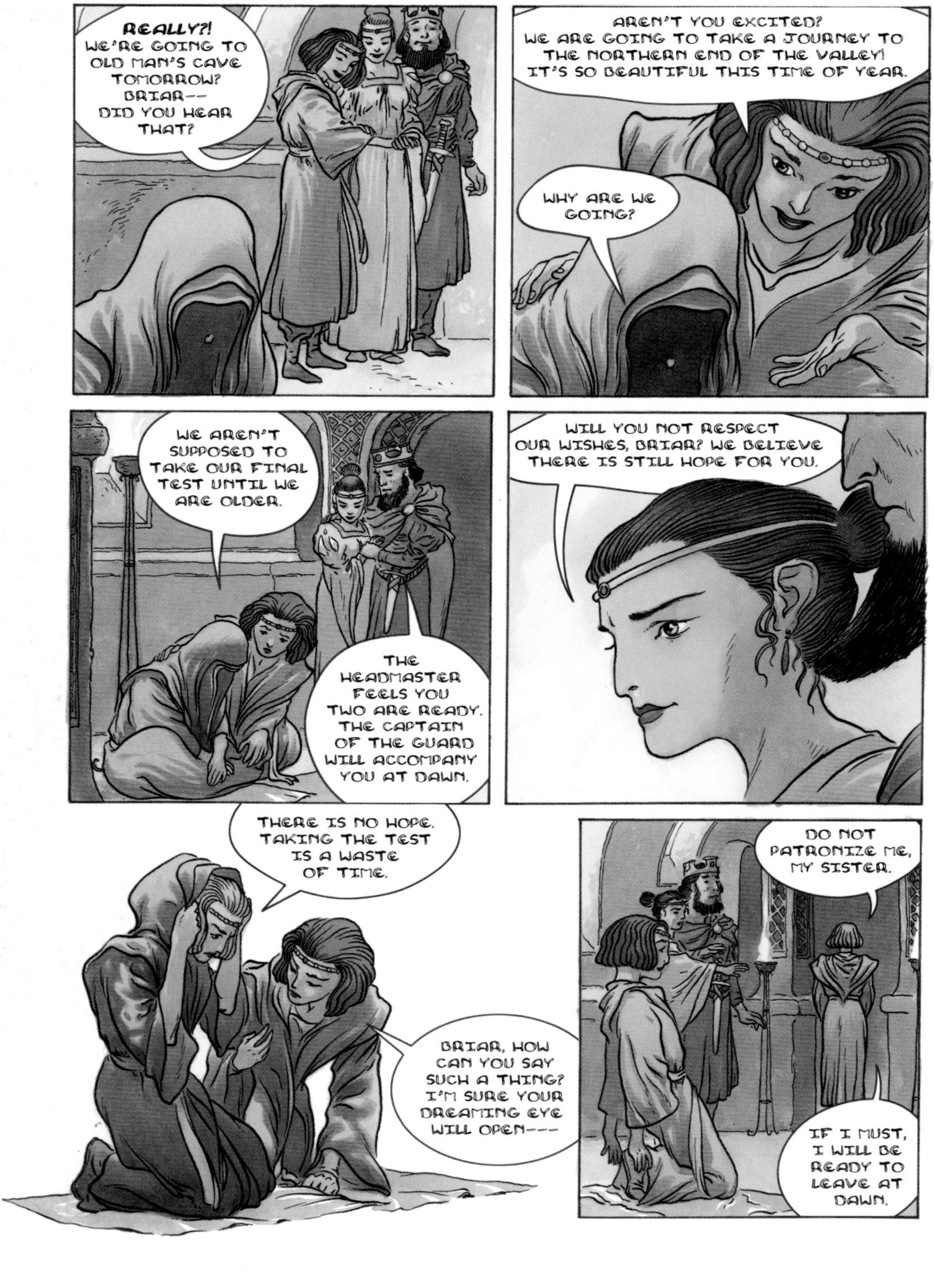
REALLY?! WE'RE GOING TO OLD MAN'S CAVE TOMORROW? BRIAR-- DID YOU HEAR THAT?
AREN'T YOU EXCITED? WE ARE GOING TO TAKE A JOURNEY TO THE NORTHERN END OF THE VALLEY! IT'S SO BEAUTIFUL THIS TIME OF YEAR.
WHY ARE WE GOING?
WE AREN'T SUPPOSED TO TAKE OUR FINAL TEST UNTIL WE ARE OLDER.
THE HEADMASTER FEELS YOU TWO ARE READY. THE CAPTAIN OF THE GUARD WILL ACCOMPANY YOU AT DAWN.
WILL YOU NOT RESPECT OUR WISHES, BRIAR? WE BELIEVE THERE IS STILL HOPE FOR YOU.
THERE IS NO HOPE. TAKING THE TEST IS A WASTE OF TIME.
BRIAR, HOW CAN YOU SAY SUCH A THING? I'M SURE YOUR DREAMING EYE WILL OPEN---
DO NOT PATRONIZE ME, MY SISTER.
IF I MUST, I WILL BE READY TO LEAVE AT DAWN.

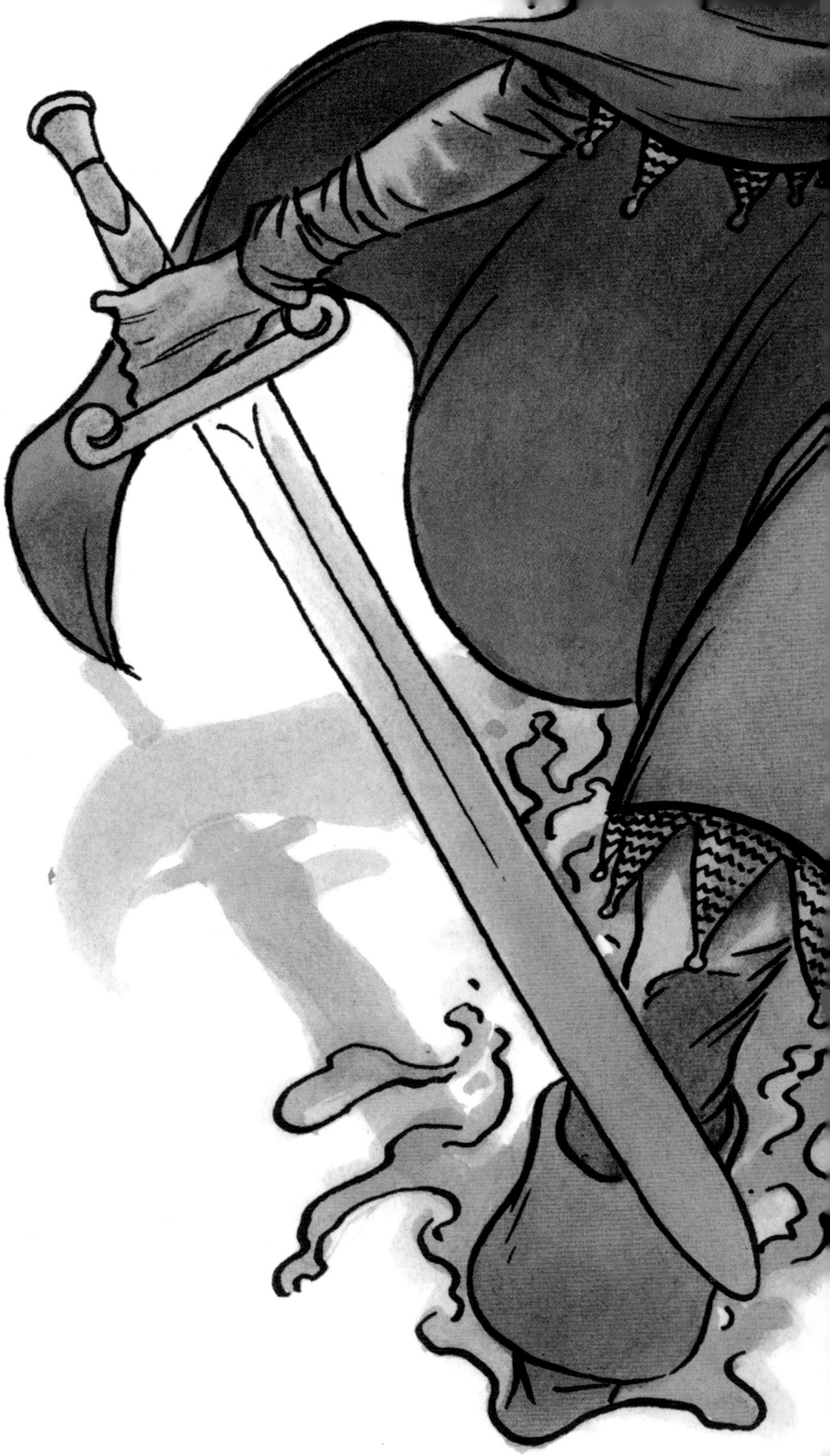

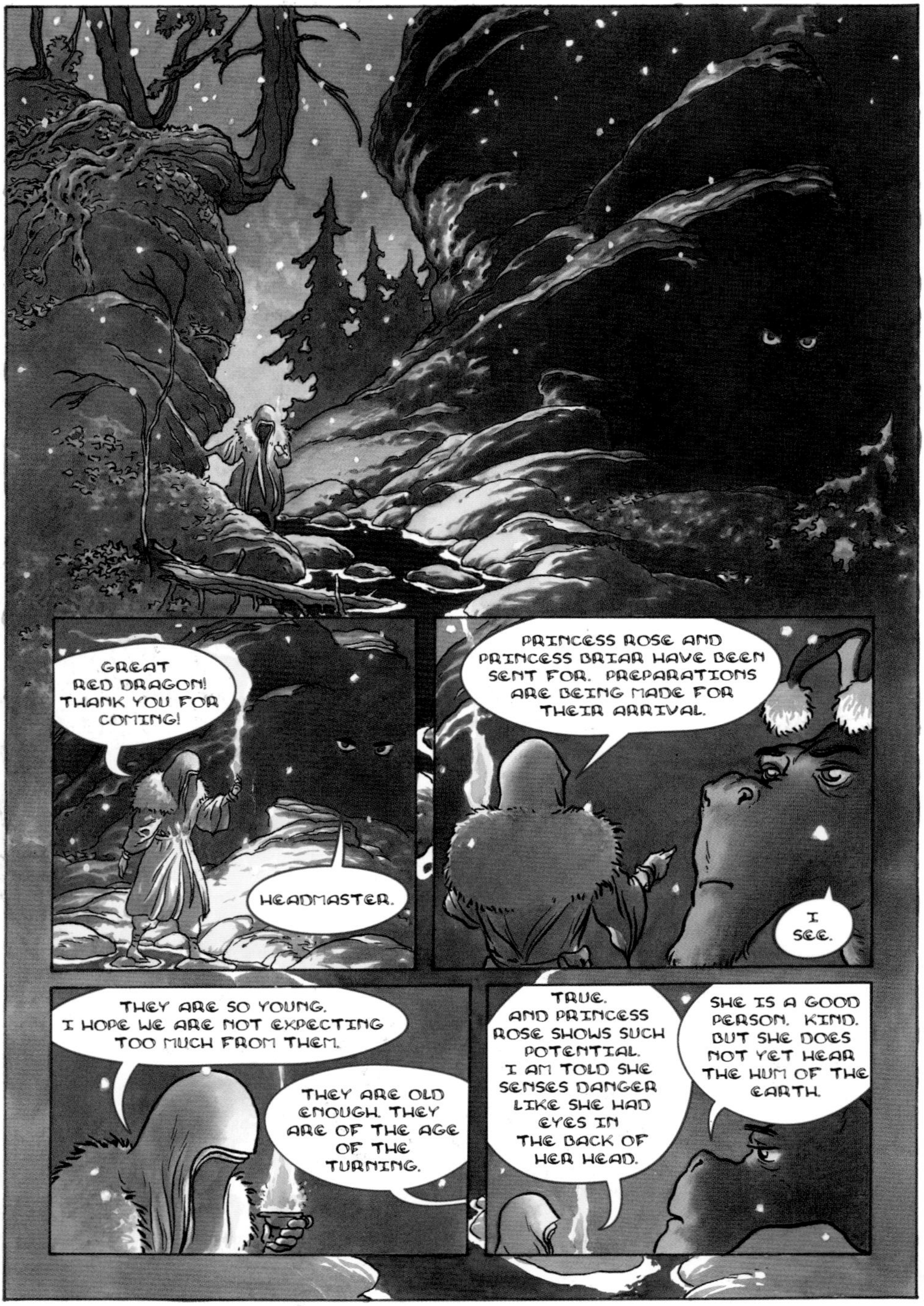
GREAT RED DRAGON! THANK YOU FOR COMING!
HEADMASTER.
PRINCESS ROSE AND PRINCESS BRIAR HAVE BEEN SENT FOR. PREPARATIONS ARE BEING MADE FOR THEIR ARRIVAL.
I SEE.
THEY ARE SO YOUNG. I HOPE WE ARE NOT EXPECTING TOO MUCH FROM THEM.
THEY ARE OLD ENOUGH. THEY ARE OF THE AGE OF THE TURNING.
TRUE. AND PRINCESS ROSE SHOWS SUCH POTENTIAL. I AM TOLD SHE SENSES DANGER LIKE SHE HAD EYES IN THE BACK OF HER HEAD.
SHE IS A GOOD PERSON. KIND. BUT SHE DOES NOT YET HEAR THE HUM OF THE EARTH.

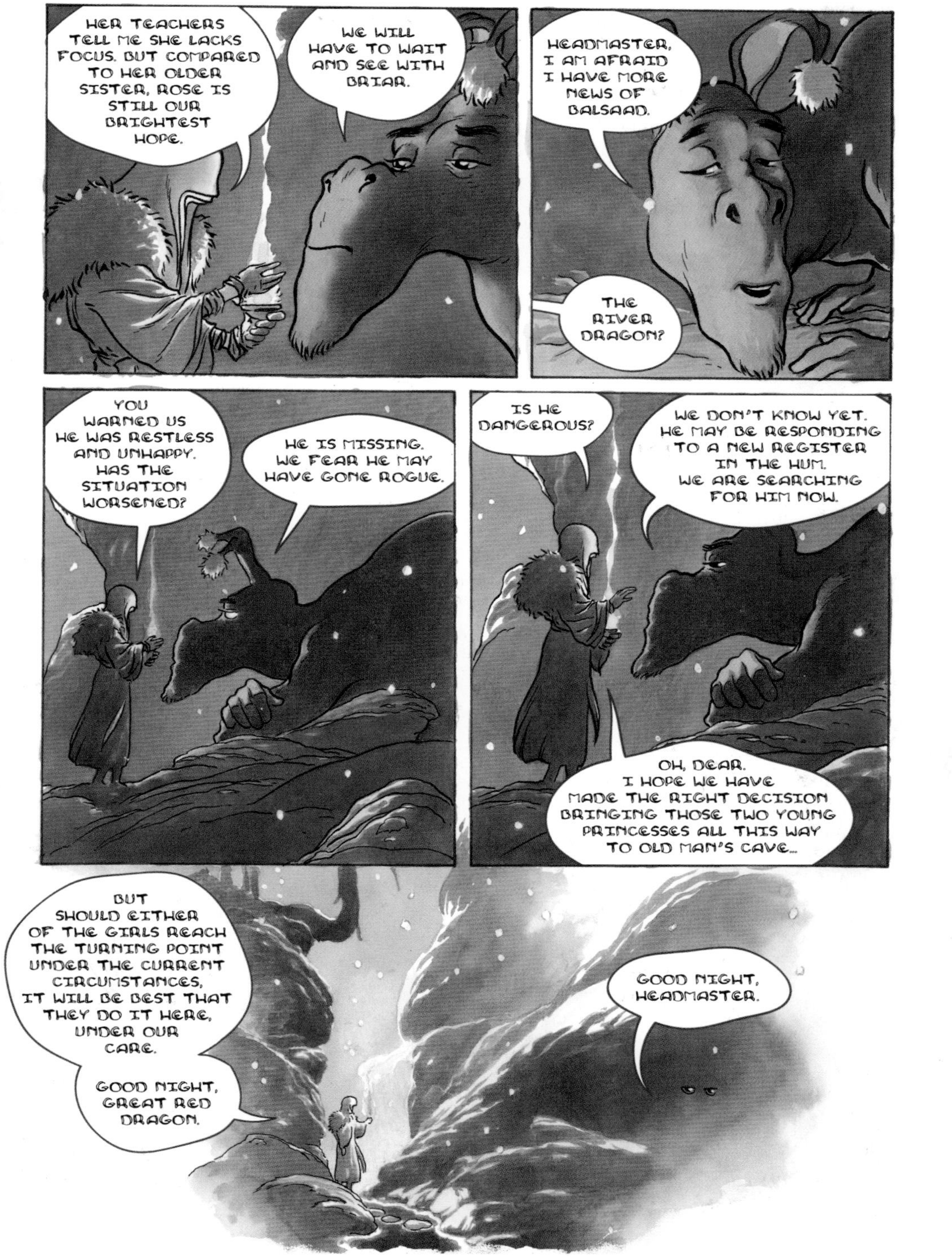
HER TEACHERS TELL ME SHE LACKS FOCUS. BUT COMPARED TO HER OLDER SISTER, ROSE IS STILL OUR BRIGHTEST HOPE.
WE WILL HAVE TO WAIT AND SEE WITH BRIAR.
HEADMASTER, I AM AFRAID I HAVE MORE NEWS OF BALSAAD.
THE RIVER DRAGON?
YOU WARNED US HE WAS RESTLESS AND UNHAPPY. HAS THE SITUATION WORSENED?
HE IS MISSING. WE FEAR HE MAY HAVE GONE ROGUE.
IS HE DANGEROUS?
WE DON'T KNOW YET. HE MAY BE RESPONDING TO A NEW REGISTER IN THE HUM. WE ARE SEARCHING FOR HIM NOW.
OH, DEAR. I HOPE WE HAVE MADE THE RIGHT DECISION BRINGING THOSE TWO YOUNG PRINCESSES ALL THIS WAY TO OLD MAN'S CAVE...
BUT SHOULD EITHER OF THE GIRLS REACH THE TURNING POINT UNDER THE CURRENT CIRCUMSTANCES, IT WILL BE BEST THAT THEY DO IT HERE, UNDER OUR CARE.
GOOD NIGHT, GREAT RED DRAGON.
GOOD NIGHT, HEADMASTER.

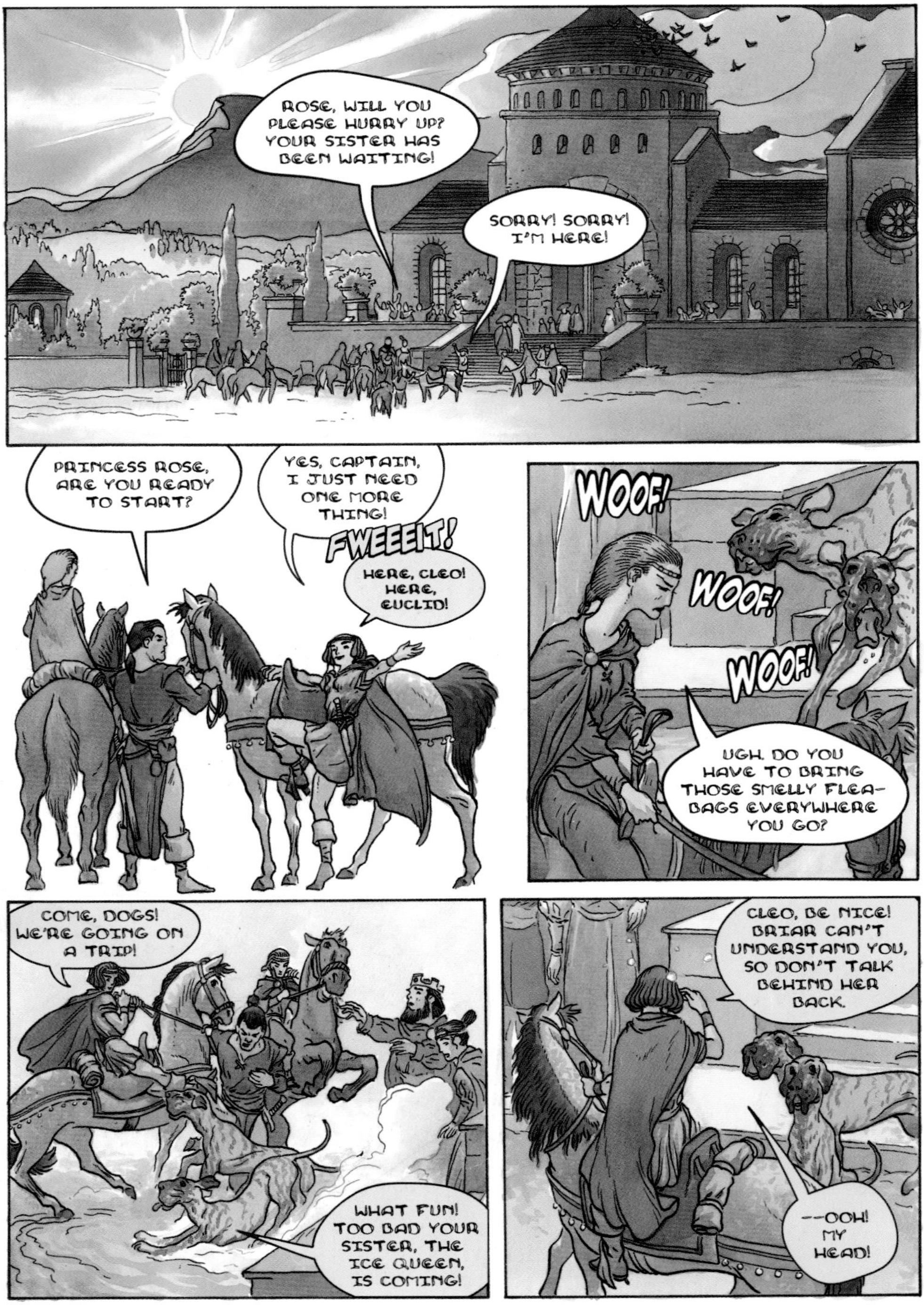
ROSE, WILL YOU PLEASE HURRY UP? YOUR SISTER HAS BEEN WAITING!
SORRY! SORRY! I'M HERE!
PRINCESS ROSE, ARE YOU READY TO START?
YES, CAPTAIN, I JUST NEED ONE MORE THING!
FWEEEIT!
HERE, CLEO! HERE, EUCLID!
WOOF!
WOOF!
WOOF!
UGH. DO YOU HAVE TO BRING THOSE SMELLY FLEA-BAGS EVERYWHERE YOU GO?
COME, DOGS! WE'RE GOING ON A TRIP!
WHAT FUN! TOO BAD YOUR SISTER, THE ICE QUEEN, IS COMING!
CLEO, BE NICE! BRIAR CAN'T UNDERSTAND YOU, SO DON'T TALK BEHIND HER BACK.
--OOH! MY HEAD!

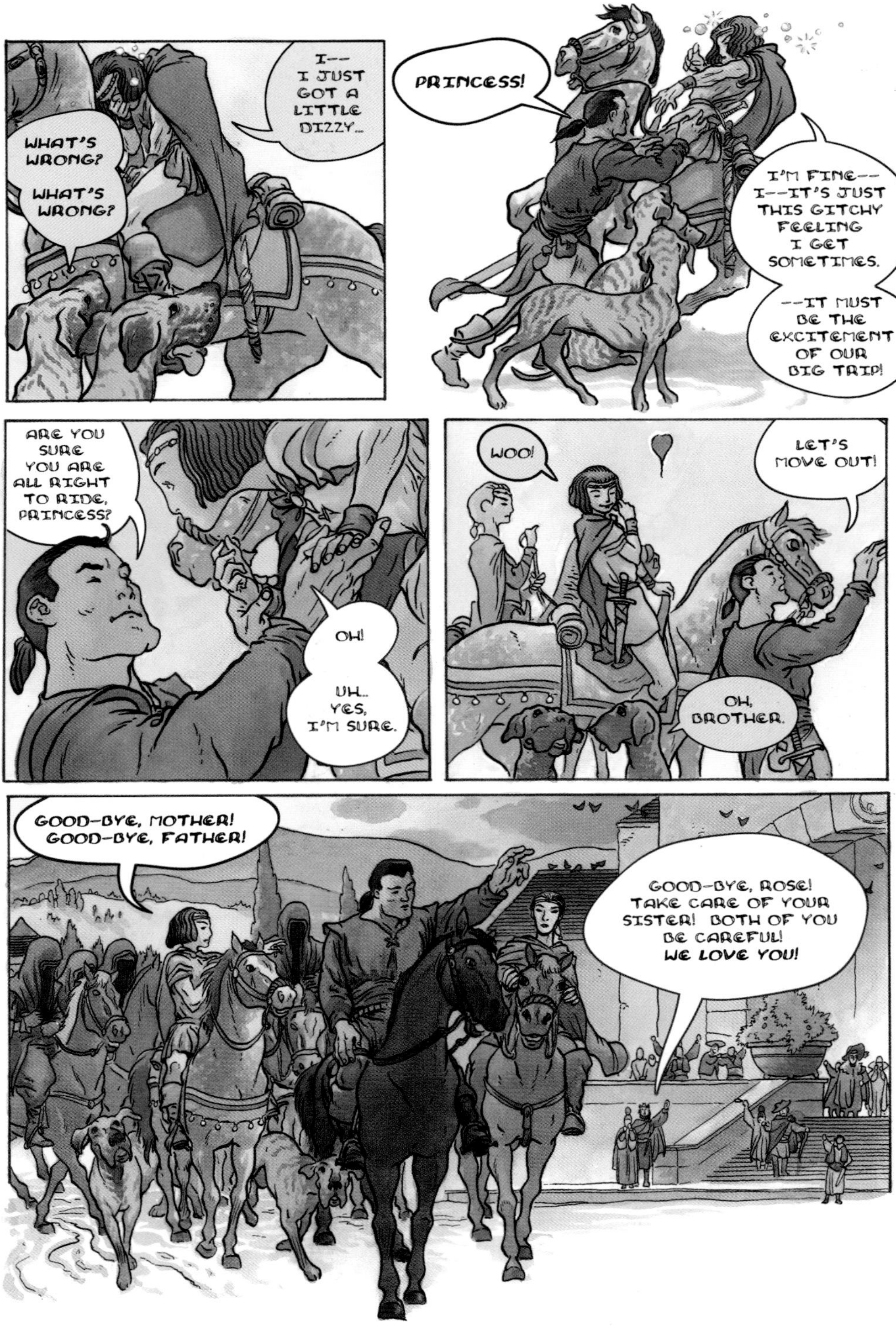
WHAT'S WRONG? WHAT'S WRONG?
I-- I JUST GOT A LITTLE DIZZY...
PRINCESS!
I'M FINE-- I--IT'S JUST THIS GITCHY FEELING I GET SOMETIMES.
--IT MUST BE THE EXCITEMENT OF OUR BIG TRIP!
ARE YOU SURE YOU ARE ALL RIGHT TO RIDE, PRINCESS?
OH!
UH... YES, I'M SURE.
WOO!
LET'S MOVE OUT!
OH, BROTHER.
GOOD-BYE, MOTHER! GOOD-BYE, FATHER!
GOOD-BYE, ROSE! TAKE CARE OF YOUR SISTER! BOTH OF YOU BE CAREFUL! WE LOVE YOU!

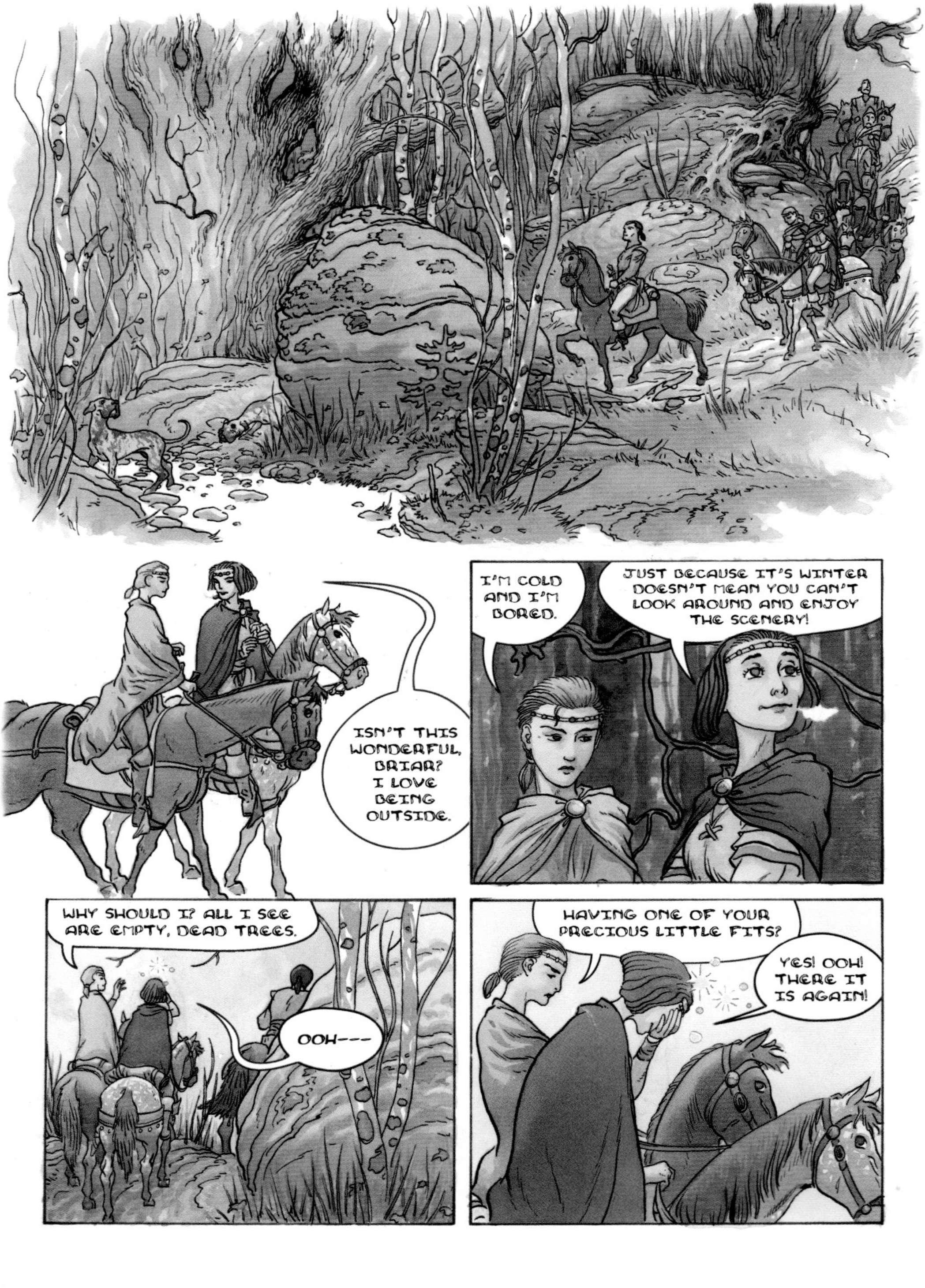
ISN'T THIS WONDERFUL, BRIAR? I LOVE BEING OUTSIDE.
I'M COLD AND I'M BORED.
JUST BECAUSE IT'S WINTER DOESN'T MEAN YOU CAN'T LOOK AROUND AND ENJOY THE SCENERY!
WHY SHOULD I? ALL I SEE ARE EMPTY, DEAD TREES.
OOH---
HAVING ONE OF YOUR PRECIOUS LITTLE FITS?
YES! OOH! THERE IT IS AGAIN!

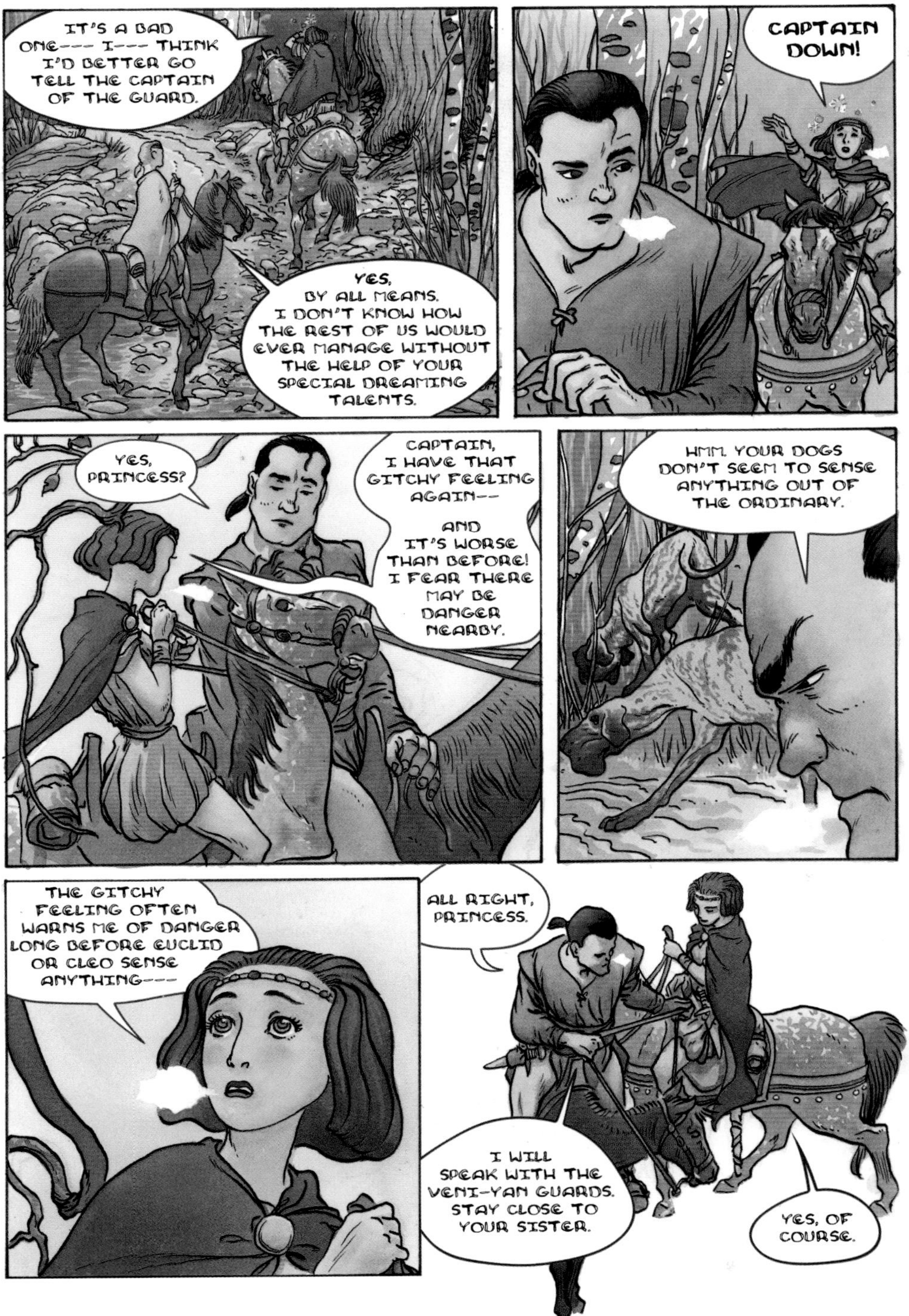
IT'S A BAD ONE--- I--- THINK I'D BETTER GO TELL THE CAPTAIN OF THE GUARD.
YES, BY ALL MEANS. I DON'T KNOW HOW THE REST OF US WOULD EVER MANAGE WITHOUT THE HELP OF YOUR SPECIAL DREAMING TALENTS.
CAPTAIN DOWN!
YES, PRINCESS?
CAPTAIN, I HAVE THAT GITCHY FEELING AGAIN--
AND IT'S WORSE THAN BEFORE! I FEAR THERE MAY BE DANGER NEARBY.
HMM. YOUR DOGS DON'T SEEM TO SENSE ANYTHING OUT OF THE ORDINARY.
THE GITCHY FEELING OFTEN WARNS ME OF DANGER LONG BEFORE EUCLID OR CLEO SENSE ANYTHING---
ALL RIGHT, PRINCESS.
I WILL SPEAK WITH THE VENI-YAN GUARDS. STAY CLOSE TO YOUR SISTER.
YES, OF COURSE.

THE PRINCESS ROSE IS WARNING US OF DANGER NEARBY. DO EITHER OF YOU SENSE ANYTHING?

I SENSE NOTHING UNUSUAL.

NOR DO I, BUT PRINCESS ROSE IS KNOWN FOR HER SKILLS IN PRESCIENCE.

BANDITS?

POSSIBLY. WE SHOULD BE WATCHFUL.

THERE IS ANOTHER DANGER... THE HAIRY MEN.

HAIRY MEN? YOU MEAN THE RAT CREATURES? WHAT WOULD THEY BE DOING THIS FAR NORTH?

THERE ARE REPORTS OF INDIVIDUALS MIGRATING NORTH ALONG THE EASTERN MOUNTAINS.

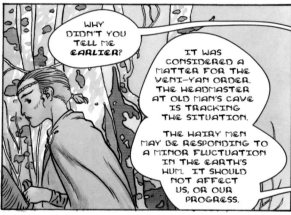

WHY DIDN'T YOU TELL ME EARLIER?

IT WAS CONSIDERED A MATTER FOR THE VENI-YAN ORDER. THE HEADMASTER AT OLD MAN'S CAVE IS TRACKING THE SITUATION.

THE HAIRY MEN MAY BE RESPONDING TO A MINOR FLUCTUATION IN THE EARTH'S HUM. IT SHOULD NOT AFFECT US, OR OUR PROGRESS.

UNLESS ONE OF THEM ATTACKS US.

IF THERE'S ANYTHING ELSE THE "ORDER" KNOWS THAT MIGHT AFFECT THE SAFETY OF OUR PRINCESSES, I EXPECT TO BE INFORMED IMMEDIATELY. UNDERSTAND?

YES, CAPTAIN.

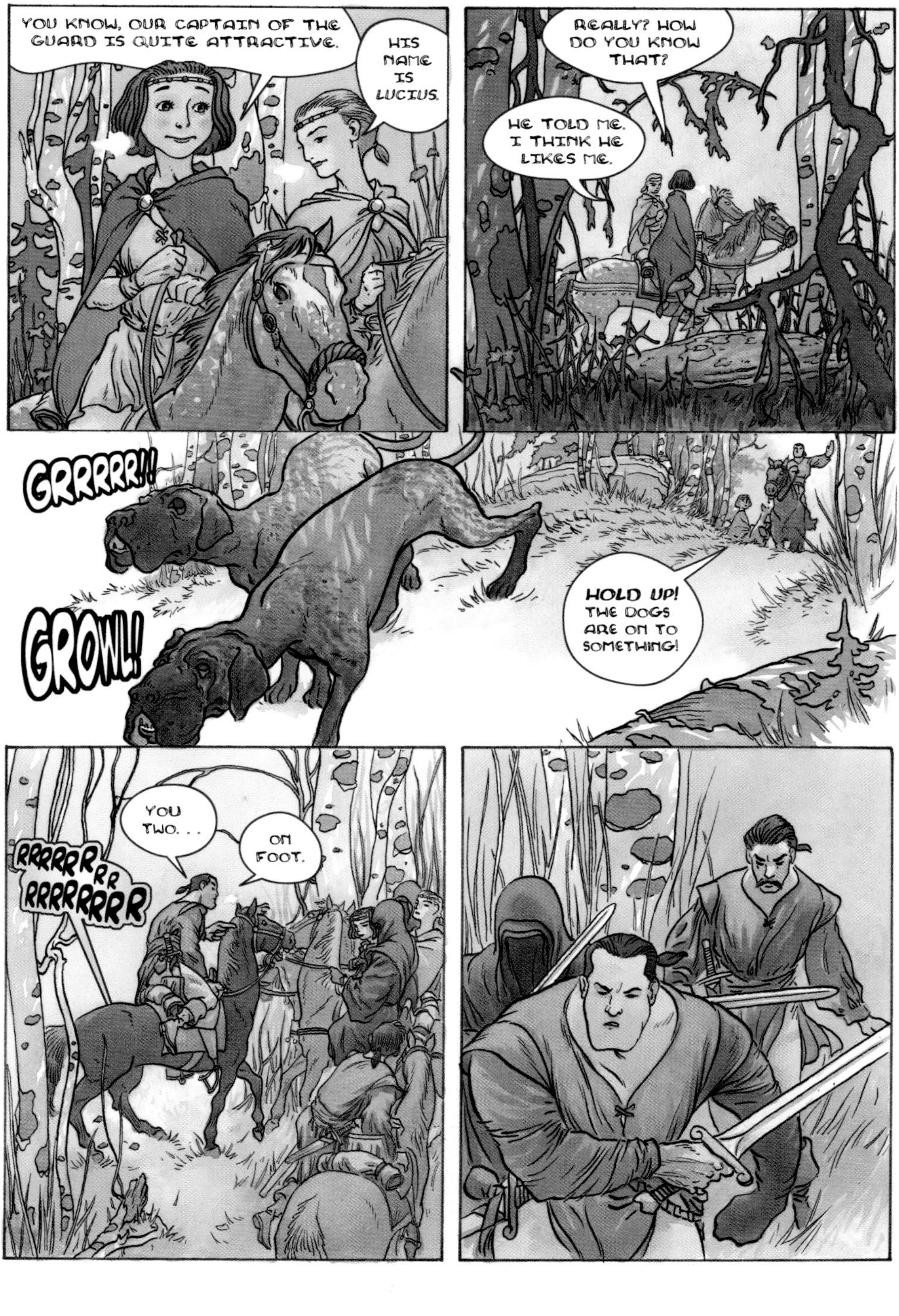
YOU KNOW, OUR CAPTAIN OF THE GUARD IS QUITE ATTRACTIVE.
HIS NAME IS LUCIUS.
REALLY? HOW DO YOU KNOW THAT?
HE TOLD ME. I THINK HE LIKES ME.
GRRRRR!!
GROWL!
HOLD UP! THE DOGS ARE ON TO SOMETHING!
RRRRRRRR RRRRRRRR
YOU TWO. . .
ON FOOT.

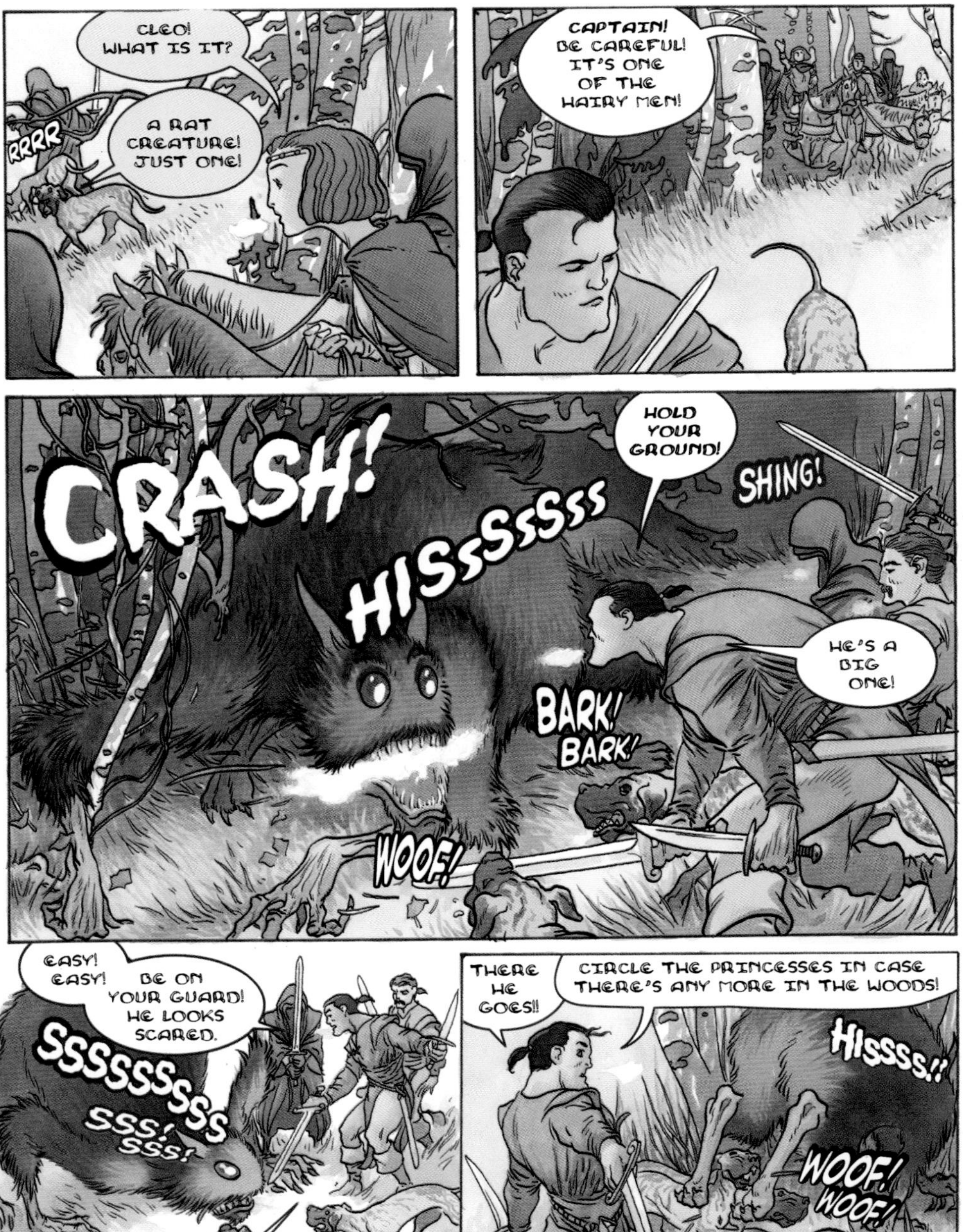
CLEO! WHAT IS IT?
RRRR
A RAT CREATURE! JUST ONE!
CAPTAIN! BE CAREFUL! IT'S ONE OF THE HAIRY MEN!
CRASH!
HISsSssss
HOLD YOUR GROUND!
SHING!
HE'S A BIG ONE!
BARK! BARK!
WOOF!
EASY! EASY!
BE ON YOUR GUARD! HE LOOKS SCARED.
SSSSSSSSSS
SSS! SSS!
HE MAY RUN!
THERE HE GOES!!
CIRCLE THE PRINCESSES IN CASE THERE'S ANY MORE IN THE WOODS!
HISSSS!!
WOOF! WOOF!

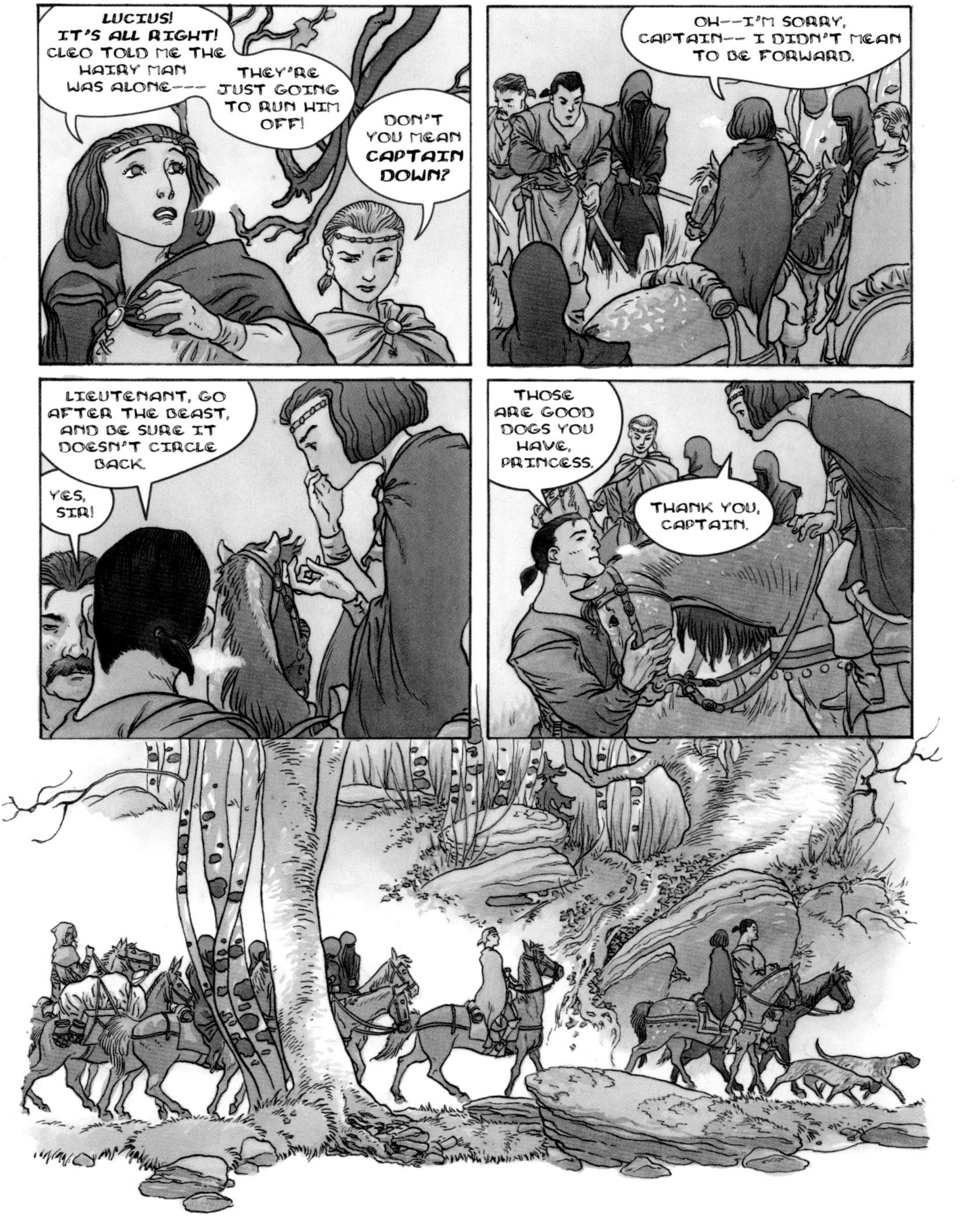
LUCIUS! IT'S ALL RIGHT! CLEO TOLD ME THE HAIRY MAN WAS ALONE---
THEY'RE JUST GOING TO RUN HIM OFF!
DON'T YOU MEAN CAPTAIN DOWN?
OH--I'M SORRY, CAPTAIN-- I DIDN'T MEAN TO BE FORWARD.
LIEUTENANT, GO AFTER THE BEAST, AND BE SURE IT DOESN'T CIRCLE BACK.
YES, SIR!
THOSE ARE GOOD DOGS YOU HAVE, PRINCESS.
THANK YOU, CAPTAIN.

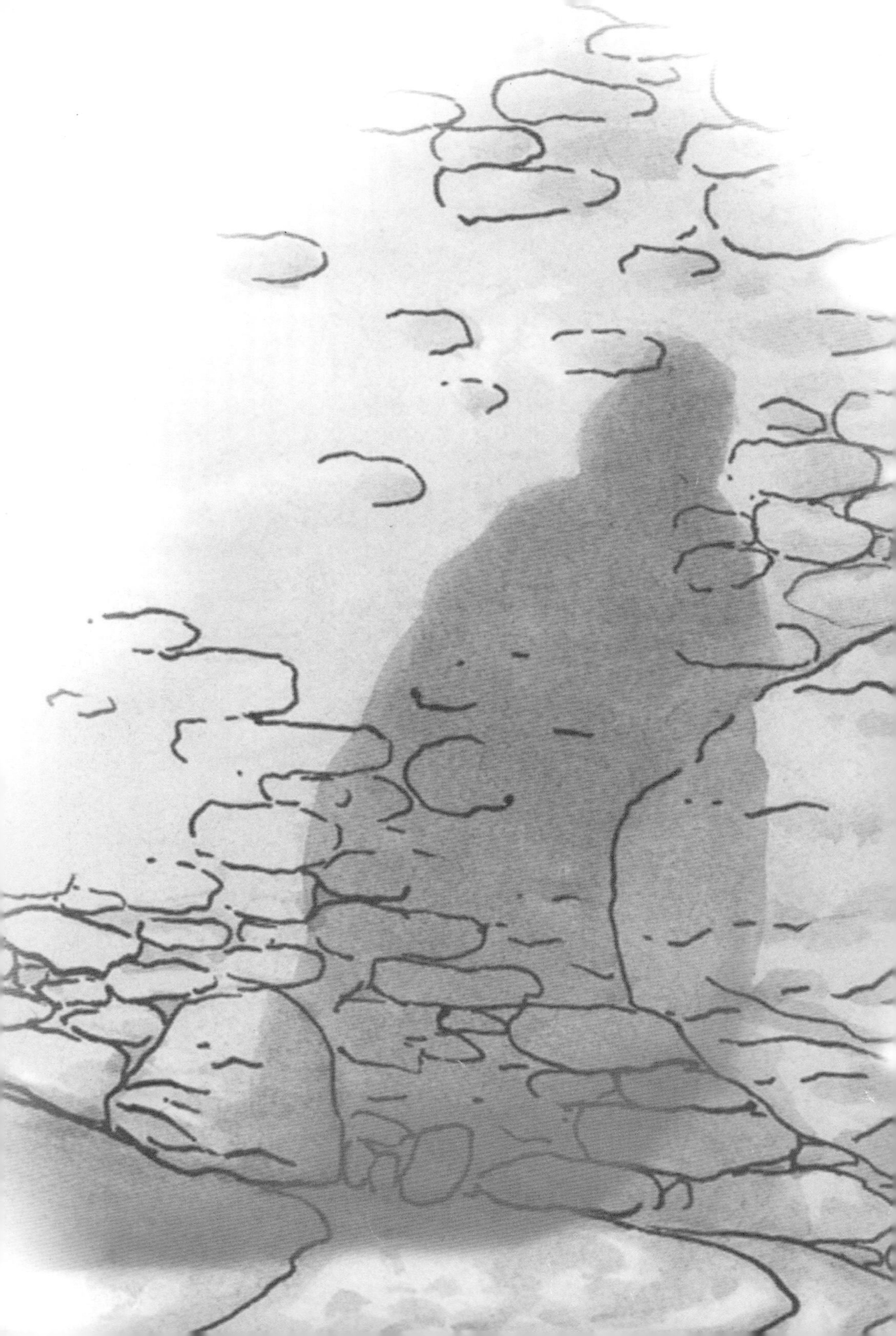

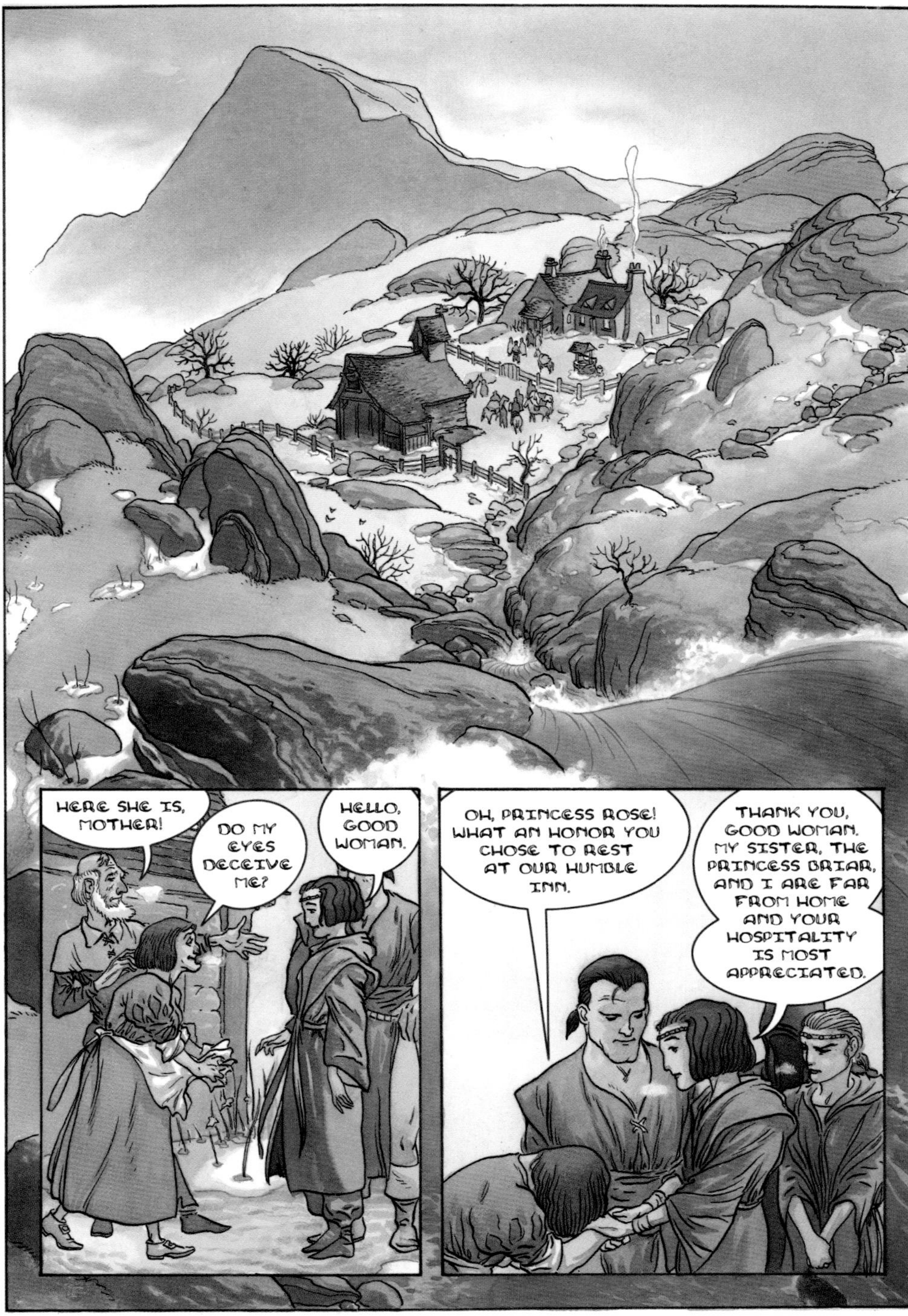
HERE SHE IS, MOTHER!
DO MY EYES DECEIVE ME?
HELLO, GOOD WOMAN.
OH, PRINCESS ROSE! WHAT AN HONOR YOU CHOSE TO REST AT OUR HUMBLE INN.
THANK YOU, GOOD WOMAN. MY SISTER, THE PRINCESS BRIAR, AND I ARE FAR FROM HOME AND YOUR HOSPITALITY IS MOST APPRECIATED.

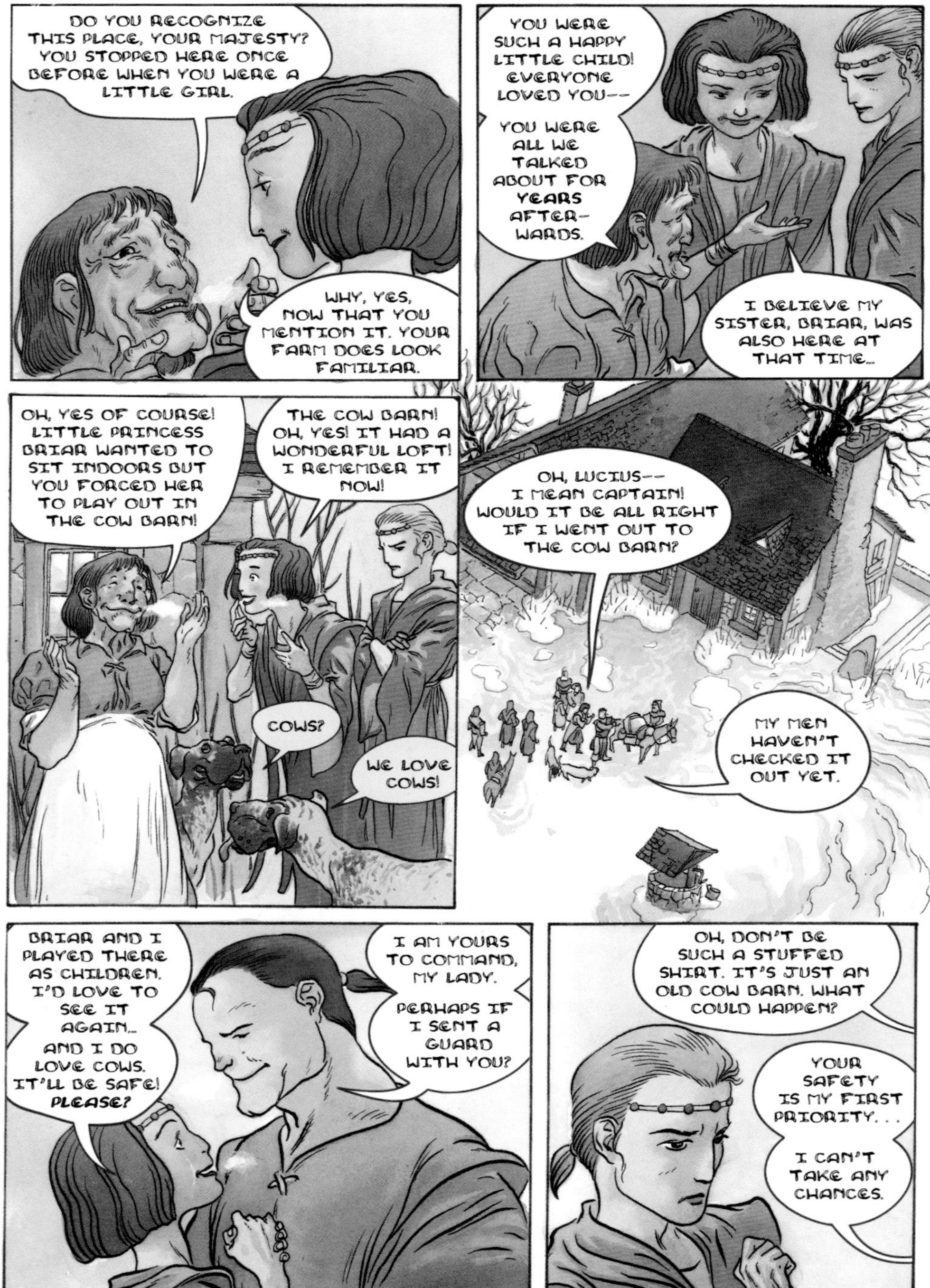
DO YOU RECOGNIZE THIS PLACE, YOUR MAJESTY? YOU STOPPED HERE ONCE BEFORE WHEN YOU WERE A LITTLE GIRL.
WHY, YES, NOW THAT YOU MENTION IT. YOUR FARM DOES LOOK FAMILIAR.
YOU WERE SUCH A HAPPY LITTLE CHILD! EVERYONE LOVED YOU--
YOU WERE ALL WE TALKED ABOUT FOR YEARS AFTER-WARDS.
I BELIEVE MY SISTER, BRIAR, WAS ALSO HERE AT THAT TIME...
OH, YES OF COURSE! LITTLE PRINCESS BRIAR WANTED TO SIT INDOORS BUT YOU FORCED HER TO PLAY OUT IN THE COW BARN!
THE COW BARN! OH, YES! IT HAD A WONDERFUL LOFT! I REMEMBER IT NOW!
COWS?
WE LOVE COWS!
OH, LUCIUS-- I MEAN CAPTAIN! WOULD IT BE ALL RIGHT IF I WENT OUT TO THE COW BARN?
MY MEN HAVEN'T CHECKED IT OUT YET.
BRIAR AND I PLAYED THERE AS CHILDREN. I'D LOVE TO SEE IT AGAIN...
AND I DO LOVE COWS. IT'LL BE SAFE! PLEASE?
I AM YOURS TO COMMAND, MY LADY.
PERHAPS IF I SENT A GUARD WITH YOU?
OH, DON'T BE SUCH A STUFFED SHIRT. IT'S JUST AN OLD COW BARN. WHAT COULD HAPPEN?
YOUR SAFETY IS MY FIRST PRIORITY. . .
I CAN'T TAKE ANY CHANCES.

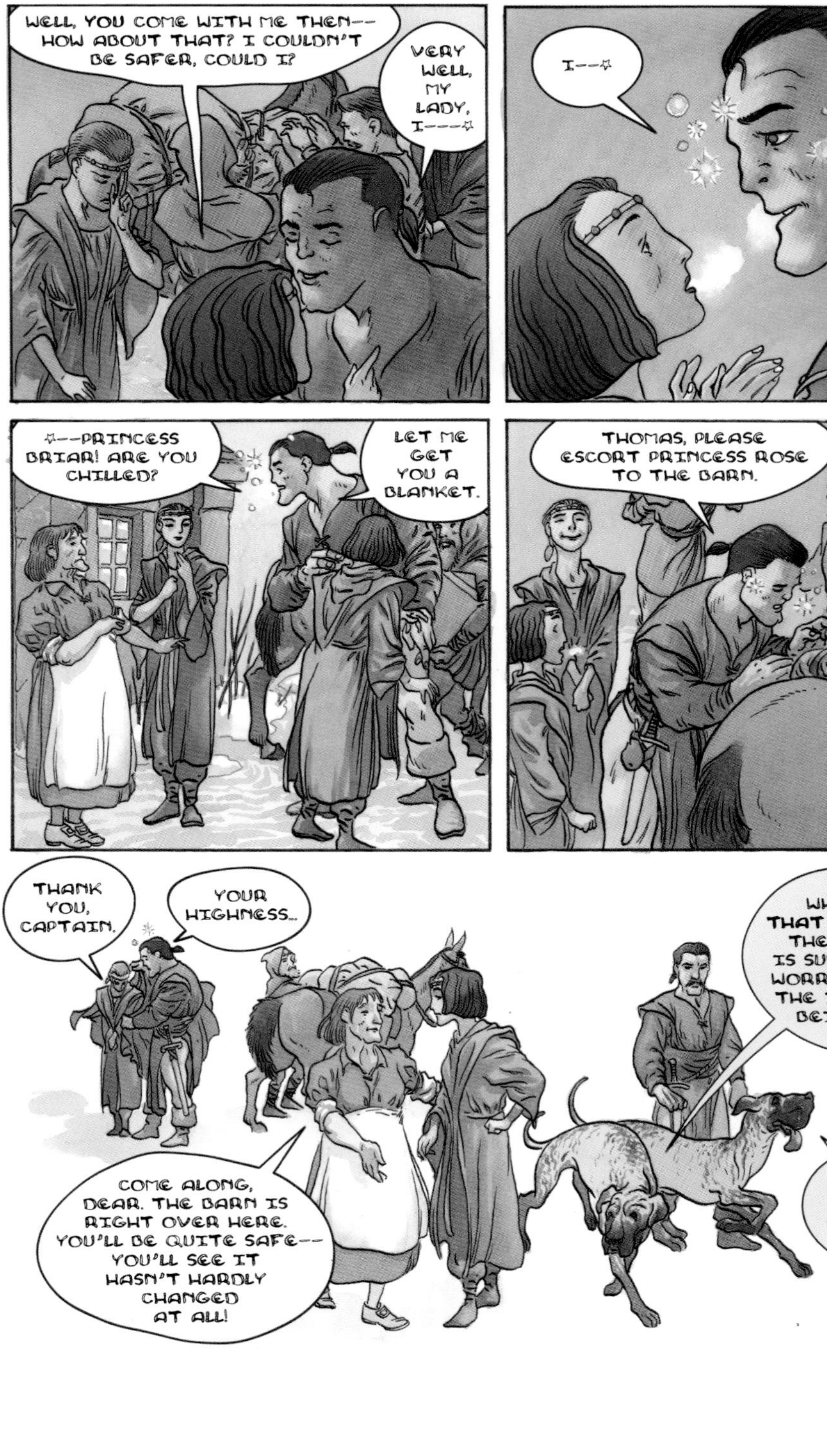
WELL, YOU COME WITH ME THEN-- HOW ABOUT THAT? I COULDN'T BE SAFER, COULD I?
VERY WELL, MY LADY, I---☆
I--☆
☆--PRINCESS BRIAR! ARE YOU CHILLED?
LET ME GET YOU A BLANKET.
THOMAS, PLEASE ESCORT PRINCESS ROSE TO THE BARN.
YES, SIR.
THANK YOU, CAPTAIN.
YOUR HIGHNESS...
WHAT WAS THAT ALL ABOUT? THE CAPTAIN IS SUDDENLY ALL WORRIED ABOUT THE ICE QUEEN BEING COLD?
COME ALONG, DEAR. THE BARN IS RIGHT OVER HERE. YOU'LL BE QUITE SAFE-- YOU'LL SEE IT HASN'T HARDLY CHANGED AT ALL!
WHO CARES! LET'S GO CHASE THE COWS!

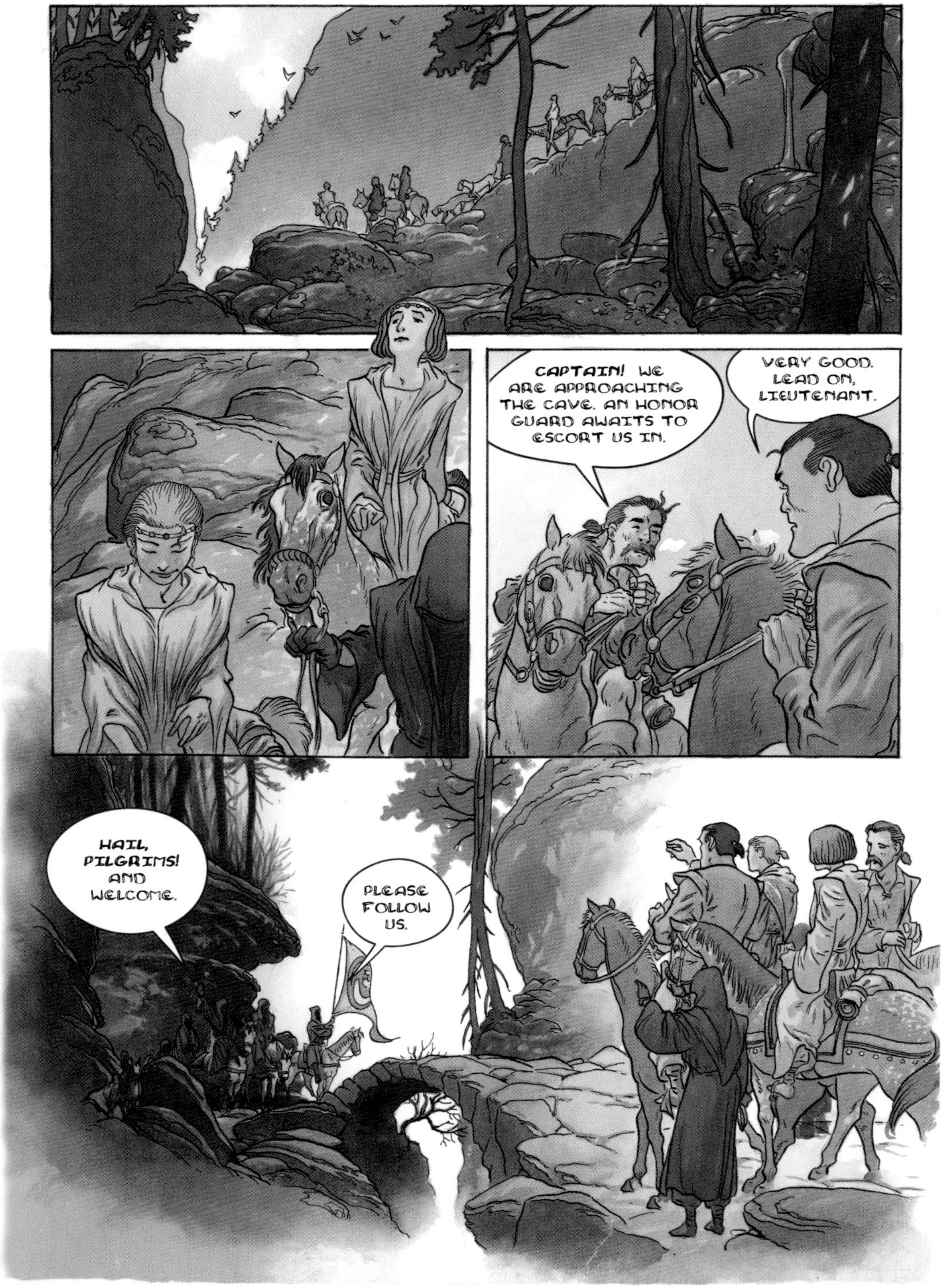
CAPTAIN! WE ARE APPROACHING THE CAVE. AN HONOR GUARD AWAITS TO ESCORT US IN.
VERY GOOD. LEAD ON, LIEUTENANT.
HAIL, PILGRIMS! AND WELCOME.
PLEASE FOLLOW US.

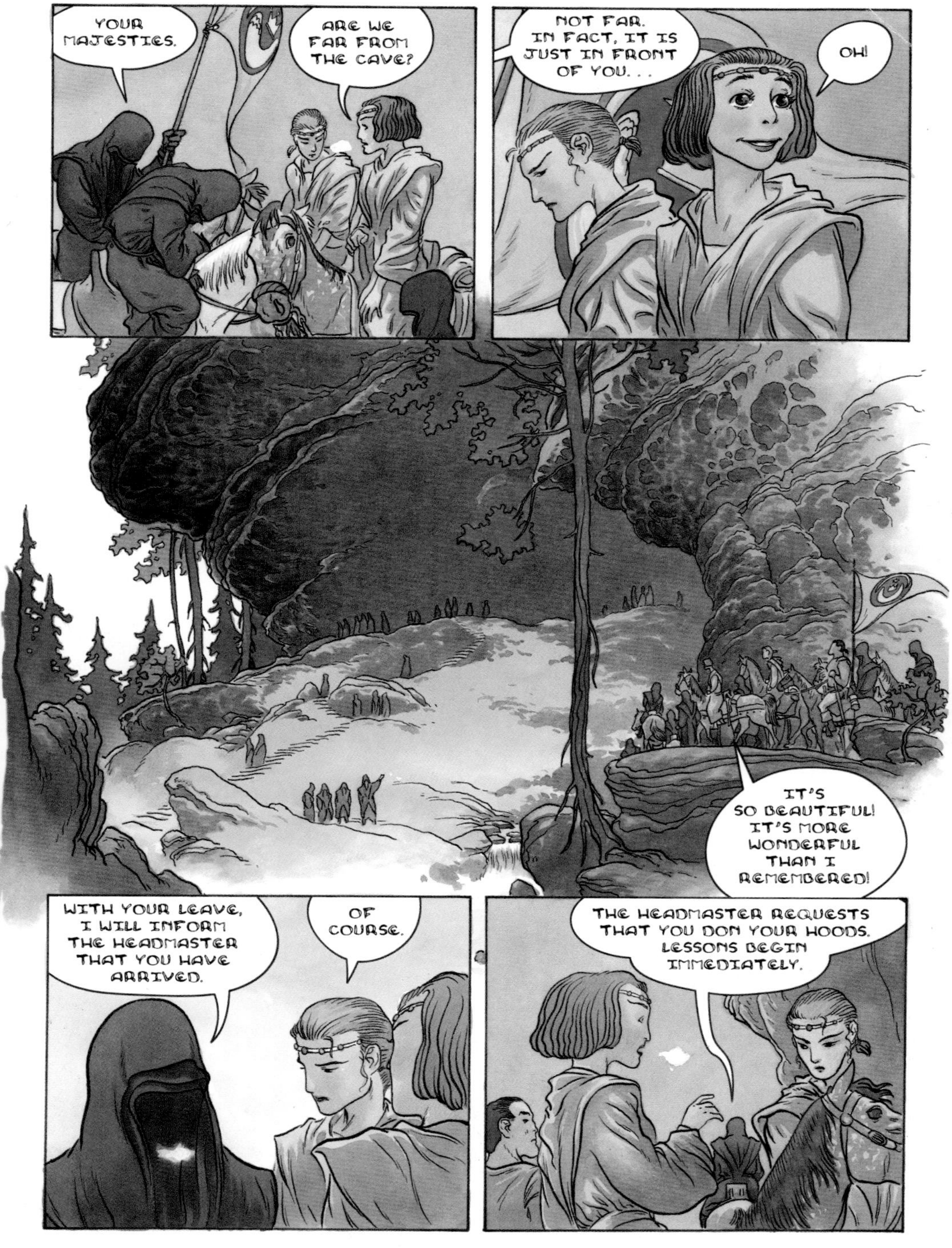
YOUR MAJESTIES.
ARE WE FAR FROM THE CAVE?
NOT FAR. IN FACT, IT IS JUST IN FRONT OF YOU. . .
OH!
IT'S SO BEAUTIFUL! IT'S MORE WONDERFUL THAN I REMEMBERED!
WITH YOUR LEAVE, I WILL INFORM THE HEADMASTER THAT YOU HAVE ARRIVED.
OF COURSE.
THE HEADMASTER REQUESTS THAT YOU DON YOUR HOODS. LESSONS BEGIN IMMEDIATELY.

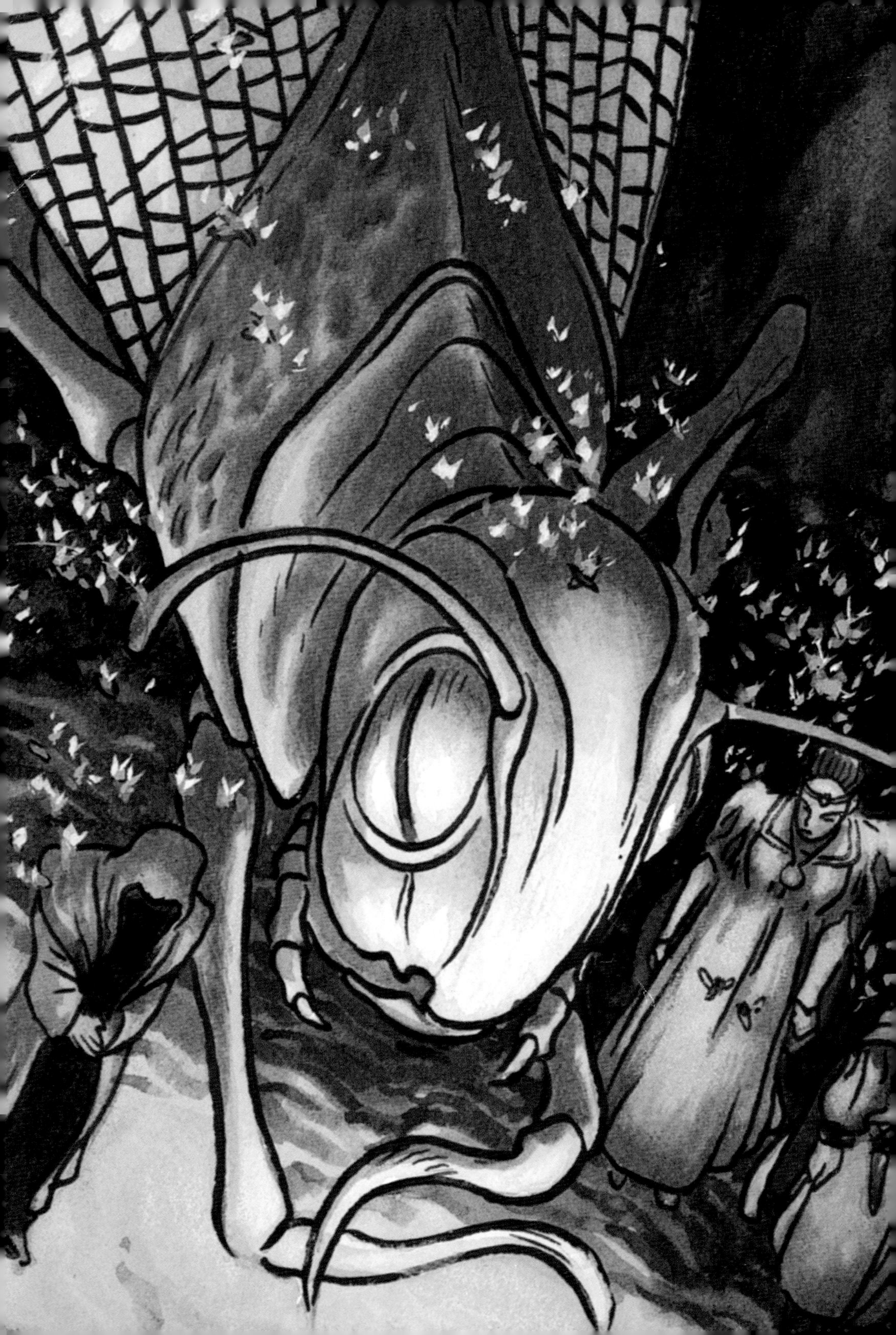

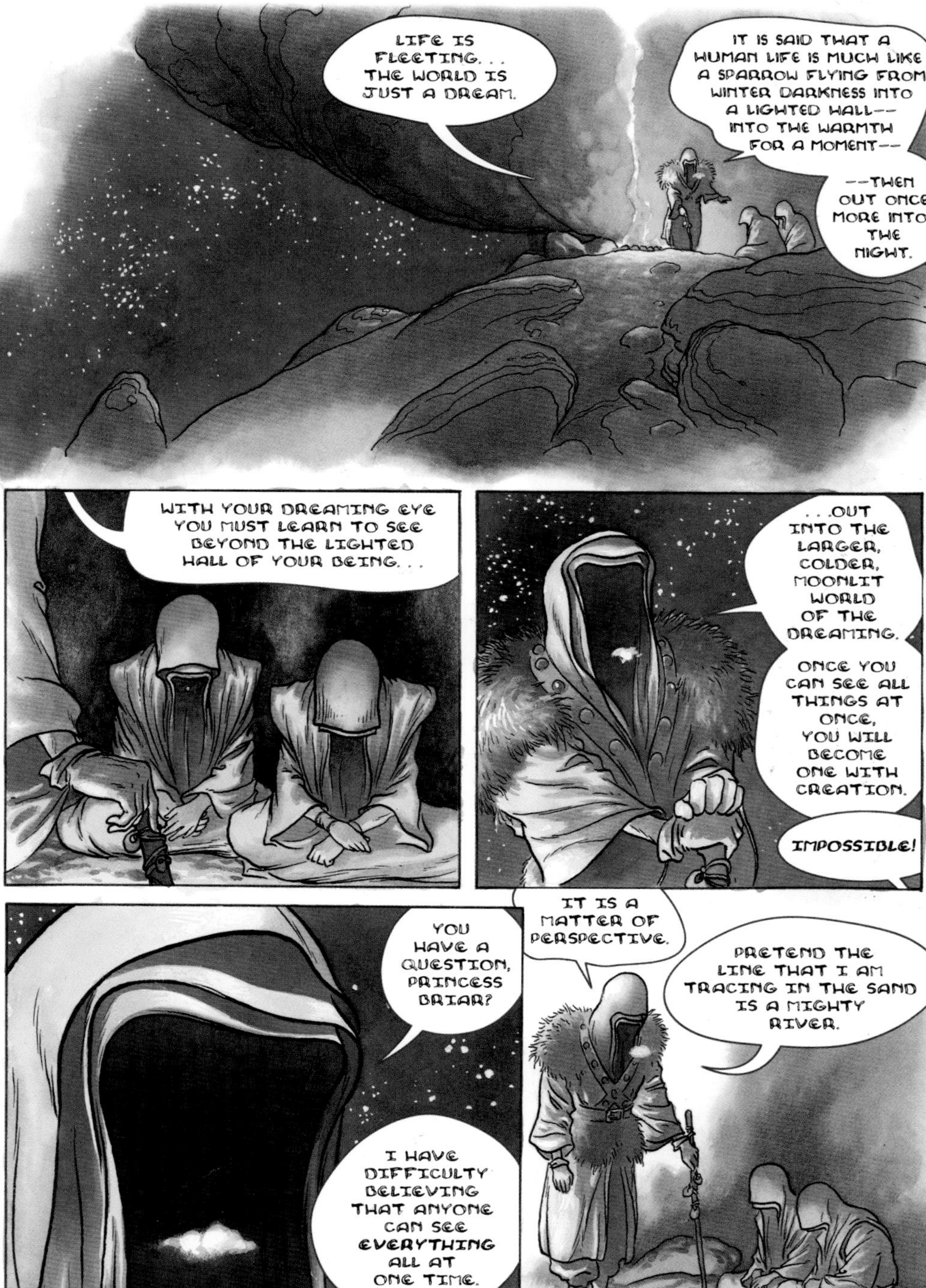
LIFE IS FLEETING. . . THE WORLD IS JUST A DREAM.
IT IS SAID THAT A HUMAN LIFE IS MUCH LIKE A SPARROW FLYING FROM WINTER DARKNESS INTO A LIGHTED HALL-- INTO THE WARMTH FOR A MOMENT--
--THEN OUT ONCE MORE INTO THE NIGHT.
WITH YOUR DREAMING EYE YOU MUST LEARN TO SEE BEYOND THE LIGHTED HALL OF YOUR BEING. . .
. . .OUT INTO THE LARGER, COLDER, MOONLIT WORLD OF THE DREAMING.
ONCE YOU CAN SEE ALL THINGS AT ONCE, YOU WILL BECOME ONE WITH CREATION.
IMPOSSIBLE!
YOU HAVE A QUESTION, PRINCESS BRIAR?
I HAVE DIFFICULTY BELIEVING THAT ANYONE CAN SEE EVERYTHING ALL AT ONE TIME.
IT IS A MATTER OF PERSPECTIVE.
PRETEND THE LINE THAT I AM TRACING IN THE SAND IS A MIGHTY RIVER.

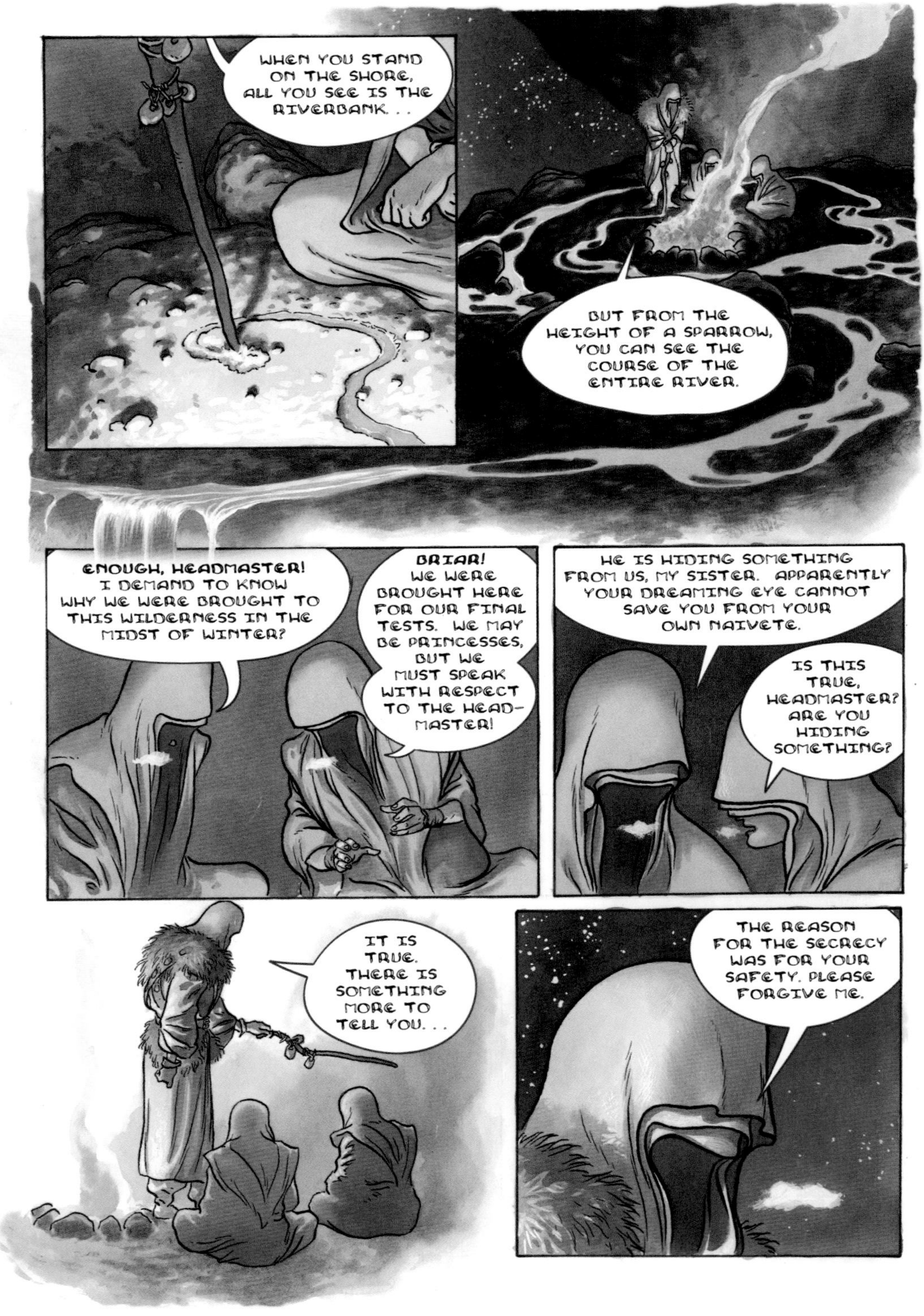
WHEN YOU STAND ON THE SHORE, ALL YOU SEE IS THE RIVERBANK. . .
BUT FROM THE HEIGHT OF A SPARROW, YOU CAN SEE THE COURSE OF THE ENTIRE RIVER.
ENOUGH, HEADMASTER! I DEMAND TO KNOW WHY WE WERE BROUGHT TO THIS WILDERNESS IN THE MIDST OF WINTER?
BRIAR! WE WERE BROUGHT HERE FOR OUR FINAL TESTS. WE MAY BE PRINCESSES, BUT WE MUST SPEAK WITH RESPECT TO THE HEAD-MASTER!
HE IS HIDING SOMETHING FROM US, MY SISTER. APPARENTLY YOUR DREAMING EYE CANNOT SAVE YOU FROM YOUR OWN NAIVETE.
IS THIS TRUE, HEADMASTER? ARE YOU HIDING SOMETHING?
IT IS TRUE. THERE IS SOMETHING MORE TO TELL YOU. . .
THE REASON FOR THE SECRECY WAS FOR YOUR SAFETY. PLEASE FORGIVE ME.

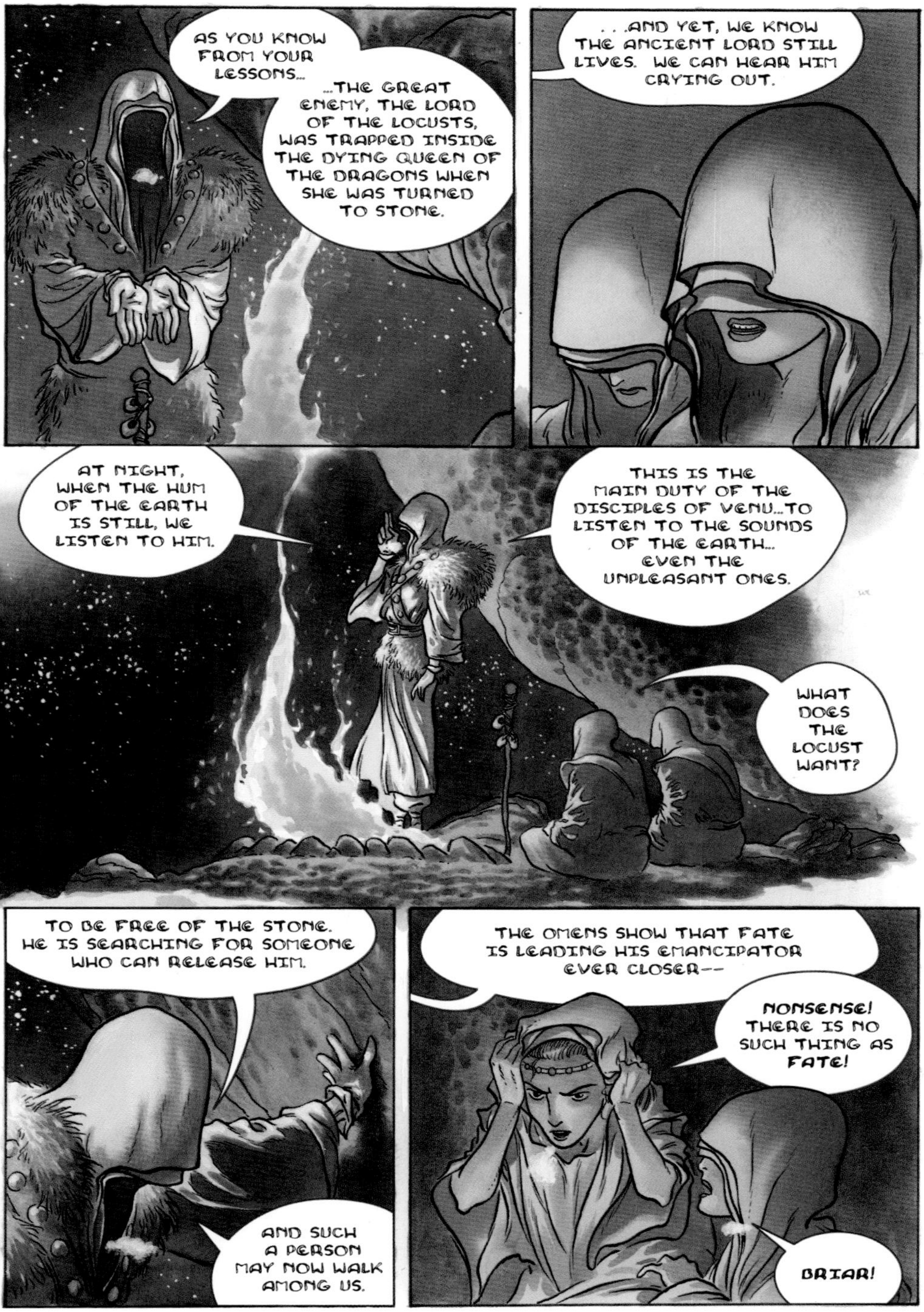
AS YOU KNOW FROM YOUR LESSONS...
...THE GREAT ENEMY, THE LORD OF THE LOCUSTS, WAS TRAPPED INSIDE THE DYING QUEEN OF THE DRAGONS WHEN SHE WAS TURNED TO STONE.
. . .AND YET, WE KNOW THE ANCIENT LORD STILL LIVES. WE CAN HEAR HIM CRYING OUT.
AT NIGHT, WHEN THE HUM OF THE EARTH IS STILL, WE LISTEN TO HIM.
THIS IS THE MAIN DUTY OF THE DISCIPLES OF VENU...TO LISTEN TO THE SOUNDS OF THE EARTH... EVEN THE UNPLEASANT ONES.
WHAT DOES THE LOCUST WANT?
TO BE FREE OF THE STONE. HE IS SEARCHING FOR SOMEONE WHO CAN RELEASE HIM.
AND SUCH A PERSON MAY NOW WALK AMONG US.
THE OMENS SHOW THAT FATE IS LEADING HIS EMANCIPATOR EVER CLOSER--
NONSENSE! THERE IS NO SUCH THING AS FATE!
BRIAR!

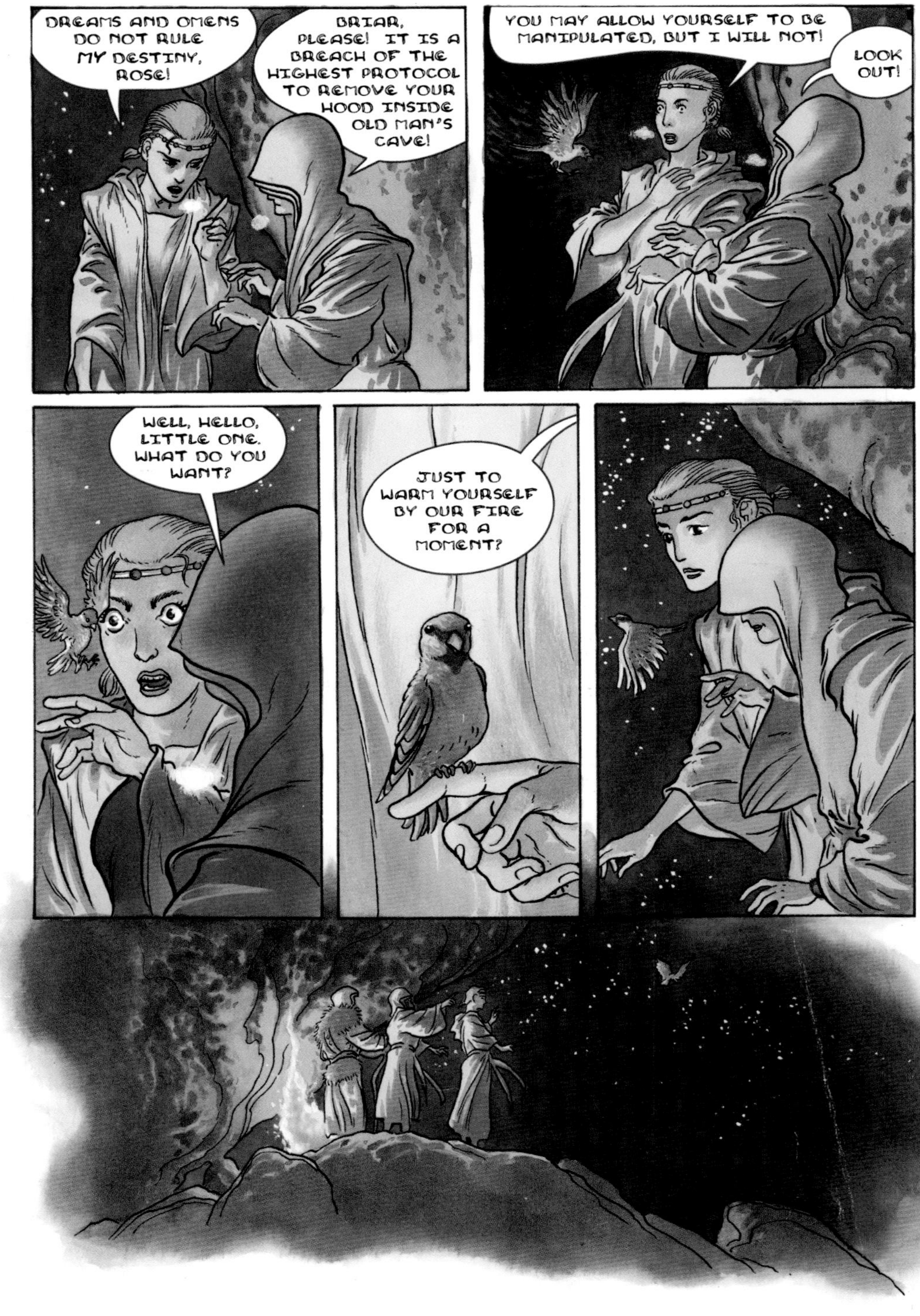
DREAMS AND OMENS DO NOT RULE MY DESTINY, ROSE!
BRIAR, PLEASE! IT IS A BREACH OF THE HIGHEST PROTOCOL TO REMOVE YOUR HOOD INSIDE OLD MAN'S CAVE!
YOU MAY ALLOW YOURSELF TO BE MANIPULATED, BUT I WILL NOT!
LOOK OUT!
WELL, HELLO, LITTLE ONE. WHAT DO YOU WANT?
JUST TO WARM YOURSELF BY OUR FIRE FOR A MOMENT?

WE ASK, TEACH

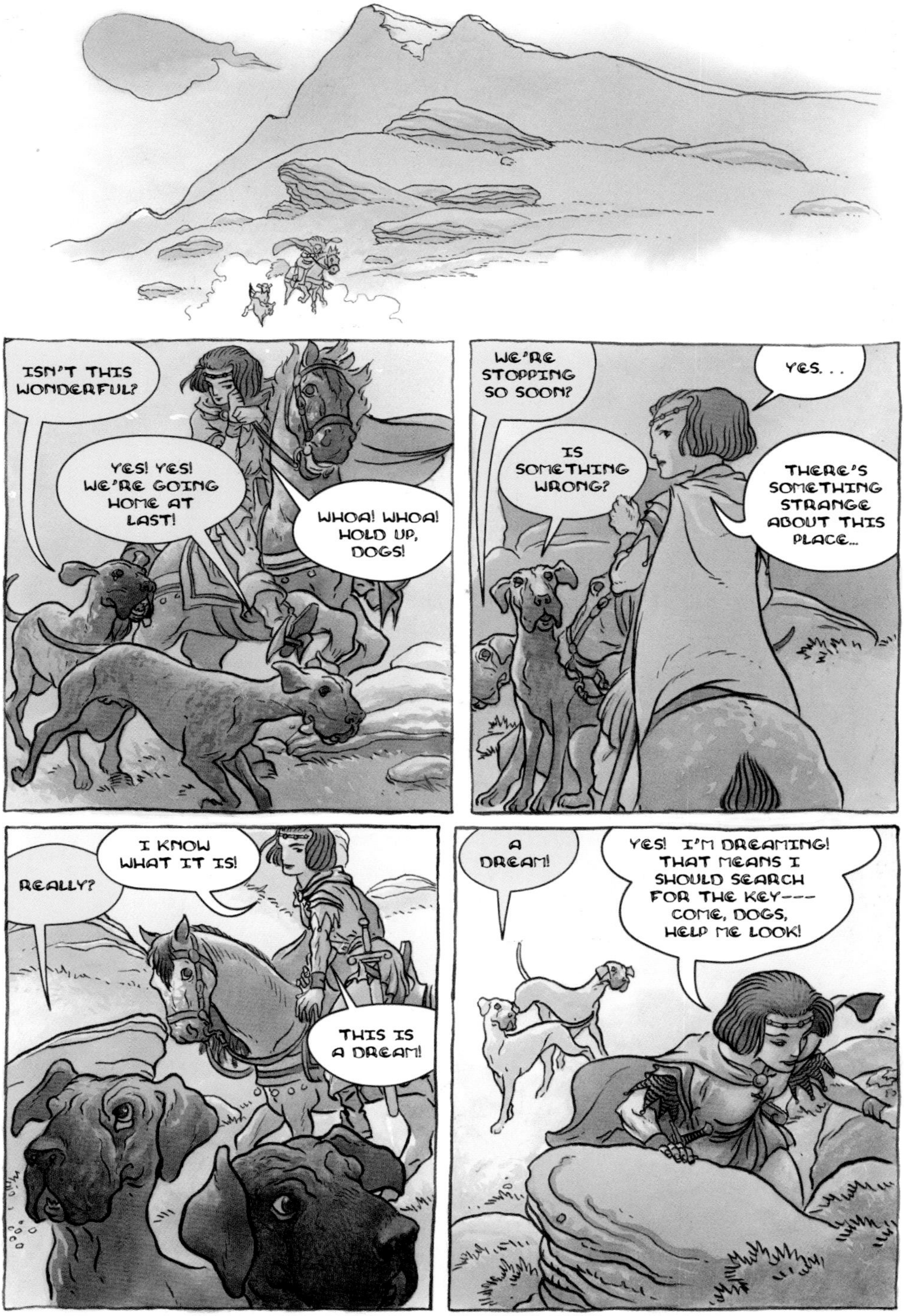

ISN'T THIS WONDERFUL?
YES! YES! WE'RE GOING HOME AT LAST!
WHOA! WHOA! HOLD UP, DOGS!
WE'RE STOPPING SO SOON?
YES. . .
IS SOMETHING WRONG?
THERE'S SOMETHING STRANGE ABOUT THIS PLACE...
REALLY?
I KNOW WHAT IT IS!
THIS IS A DREAM!
A DREAM!
YES! I'M DREAMING! THAT MEANS I SHOULD SEARCH FOR THE KEY--- COME, DOGS, HELP ME LOOK!

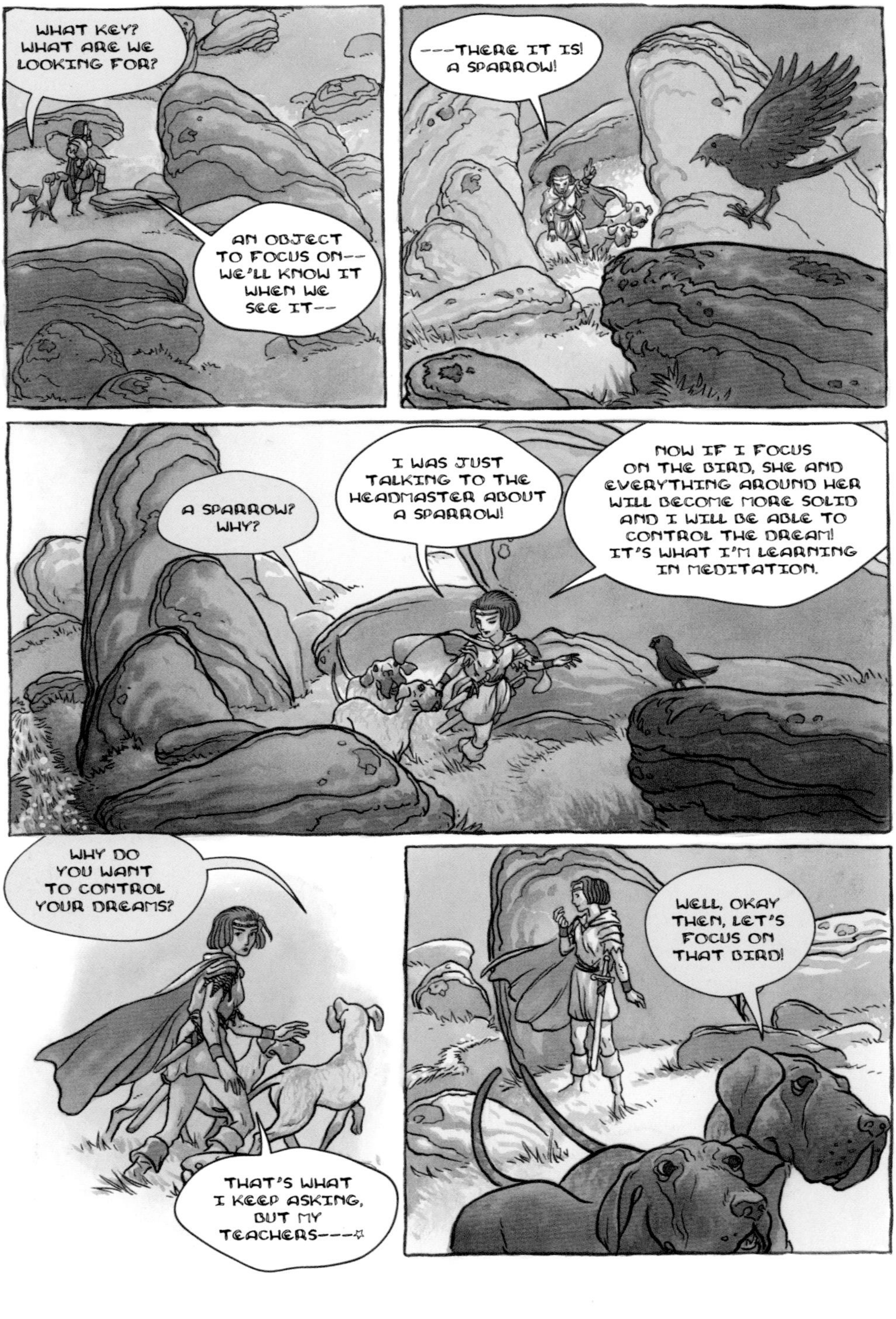
WHAT KEY? WHAT ARE WE LOOKING FOR?
AN OBJECT TO FOCUS ON-- WE'LL KNOW IT WHEN WE SEE IT--
---THERE IT IS! A SPARROW!
A SPARROW? WHY?
I WAS JUST TALKING TO THE HEADMASTER ABOUT A SPARROW!
NOW IF I FOCUS ON THE BIRD, SHE AND EVERYTHING AROUND HER WILL BECOME MORE SOLID AND I WILL BE ABLE TO CONTROL THE DREAM! IT'S WHAT I'M LEARNING IN MEDITATION.
WHY DO YOU WANT TO CONTROL YOUR DREAMS?
THAT'S WHAT I KEEP ASKING, BUT MY TEACHERS---☆
WELL, OKAY THEN, LET'S FOCUS ON THAT BIRD!

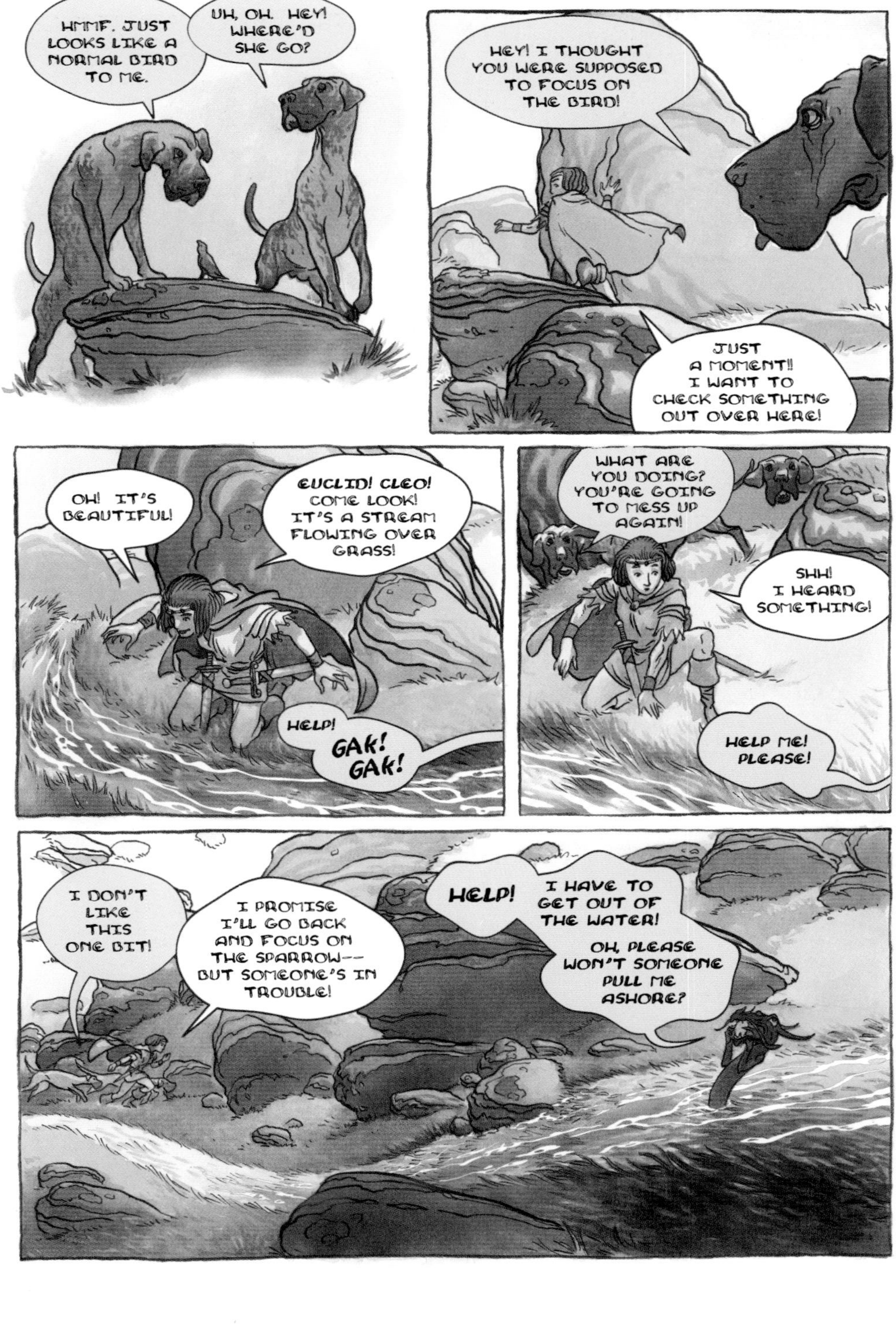
HMMF. JUST LOOKS LIKE A NORMAL BIRD TO ME.
UH, OH. HEY! WHERE'D SHE GO?
HEY! I THOUGHT YOU WERE SUPPOSED TO FOCUS ON THE BIRD!
JUST A MOMENT!! I WANT TO CHECK SOMETHING OUT OVER HERE!
OH! IT'S BEAUTIFUL!
EUCLID! CLEO! COME LOOK! IT'S A STREAM FLOWING OVER GRASS!
HELP!
GAK! GAK!
WHAT ARE YOU DOING? YOU'RE GOING TO MESS UP AGAIN!
SHH! I HEARD SOMETHING!
HELP ME! PLEASE!
I DON'T LIKE THIS ONE BIT!
I PROMISE I'LL GO BACK AND FOCUS ON THE SPARROW-- BUT SOMEONE'S IN TROUBLE!
HELP!
I HAVE TO GET OUT OF THE WATER!
OH, PLEASE WON'T SOMEONE PULL ME ASHORE?

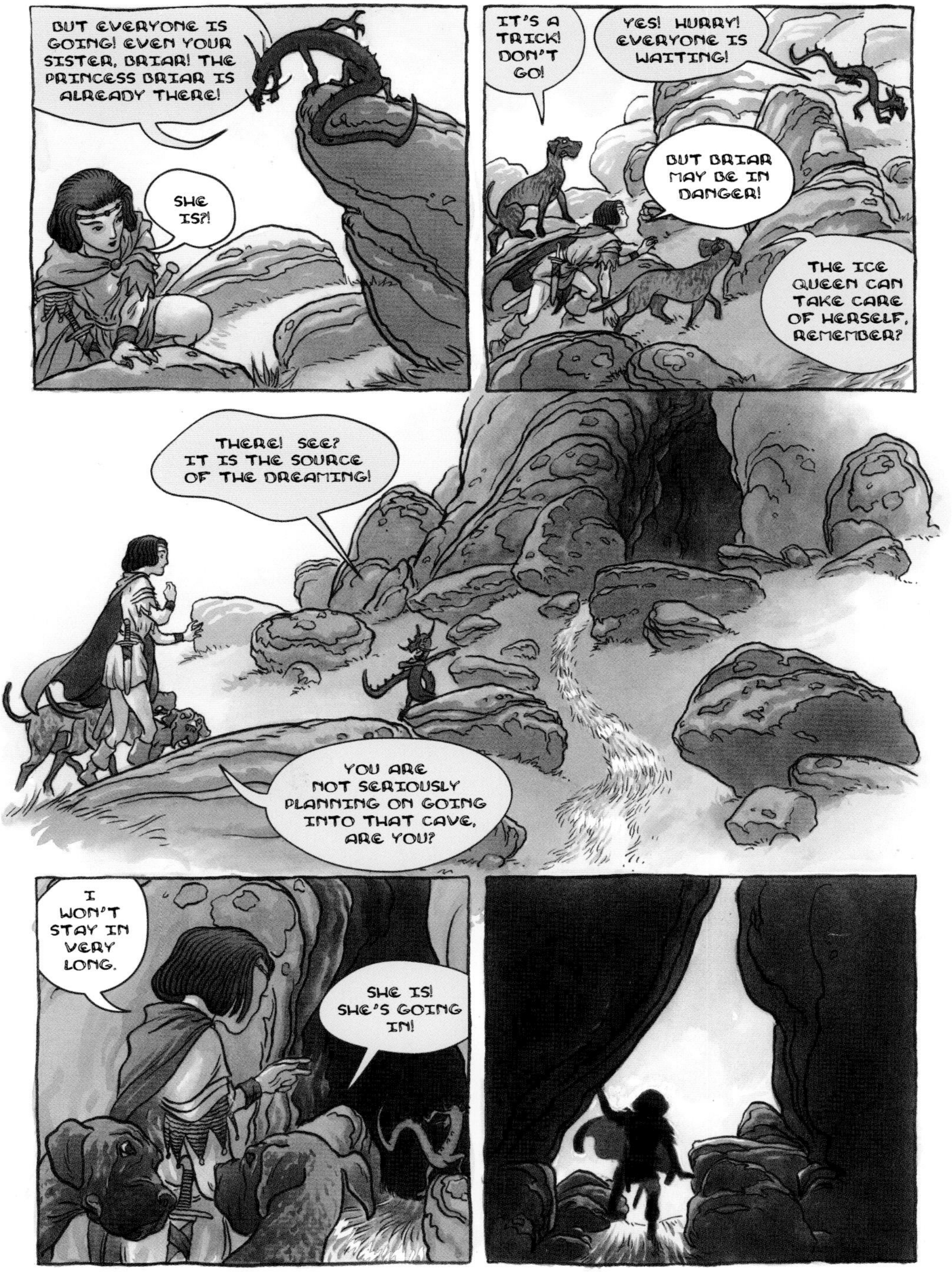
BUT EVERYONE IS GOING! EVEN YOUR SISTER, BRIAR! THE PRINCESS BRIAR IS ALREADY THERE!
SHE IS?!
IT'S A TRICK! DON'T GO!
YES! HURRY! EVERYONE IS WAITING!
BUT BRIAR MAY BE IN DANGER!
THE ICE QUEEN CAN TAKE CARE OF HERSELF, REMEMBER?
THERE! SEE? IT IS THE SOURCE OF THE DREAMING!
YOU ARE NOT SERIOUSLY PLANNING ON GOING INTO THAT CAVE, ARE YOU?
I WON'T STAY IN VERY LONG.
SHE IS! SHE'S GOING IN!

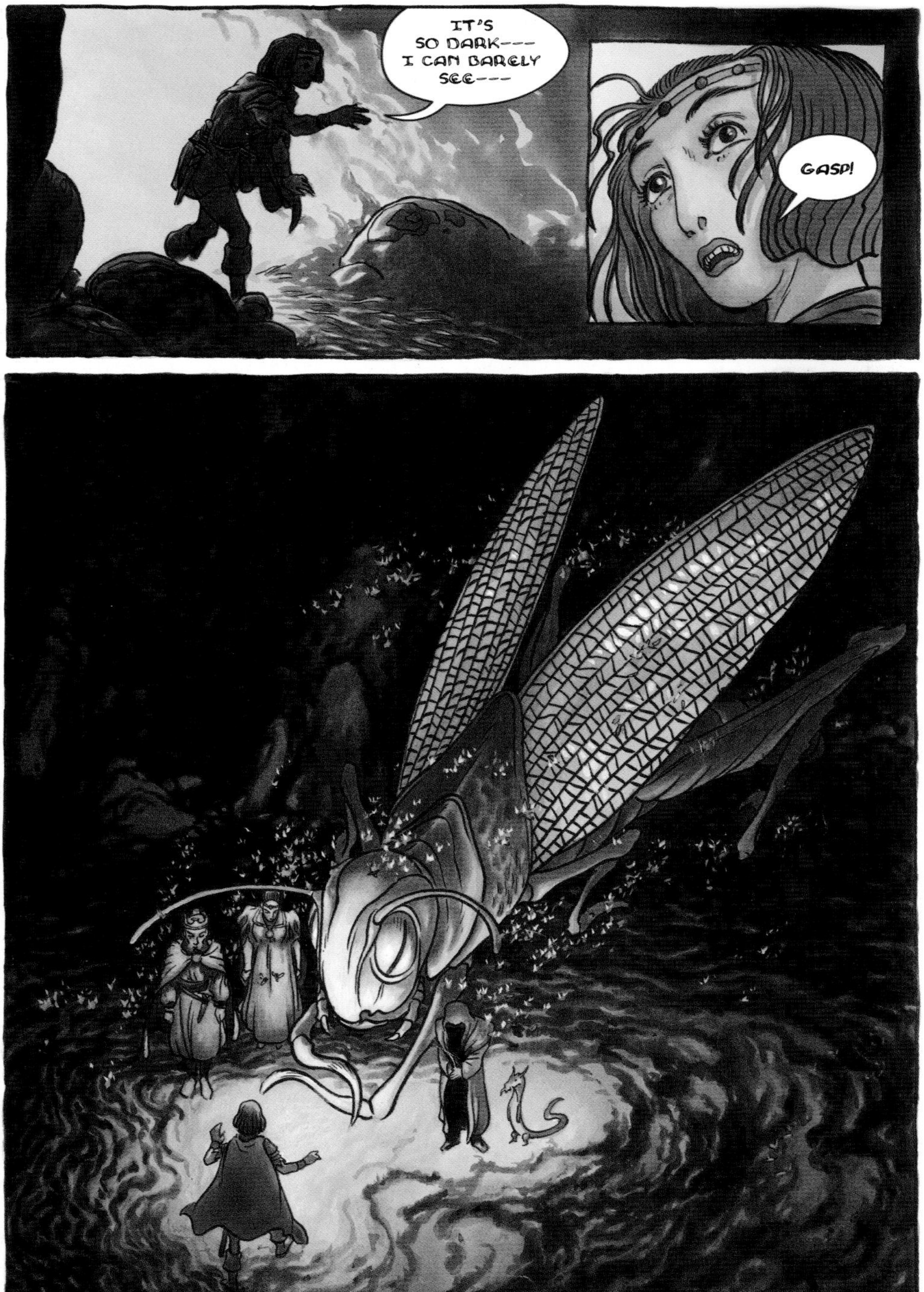
IT'S SO DARK--- I CAN BARELY SEE---
GASP!

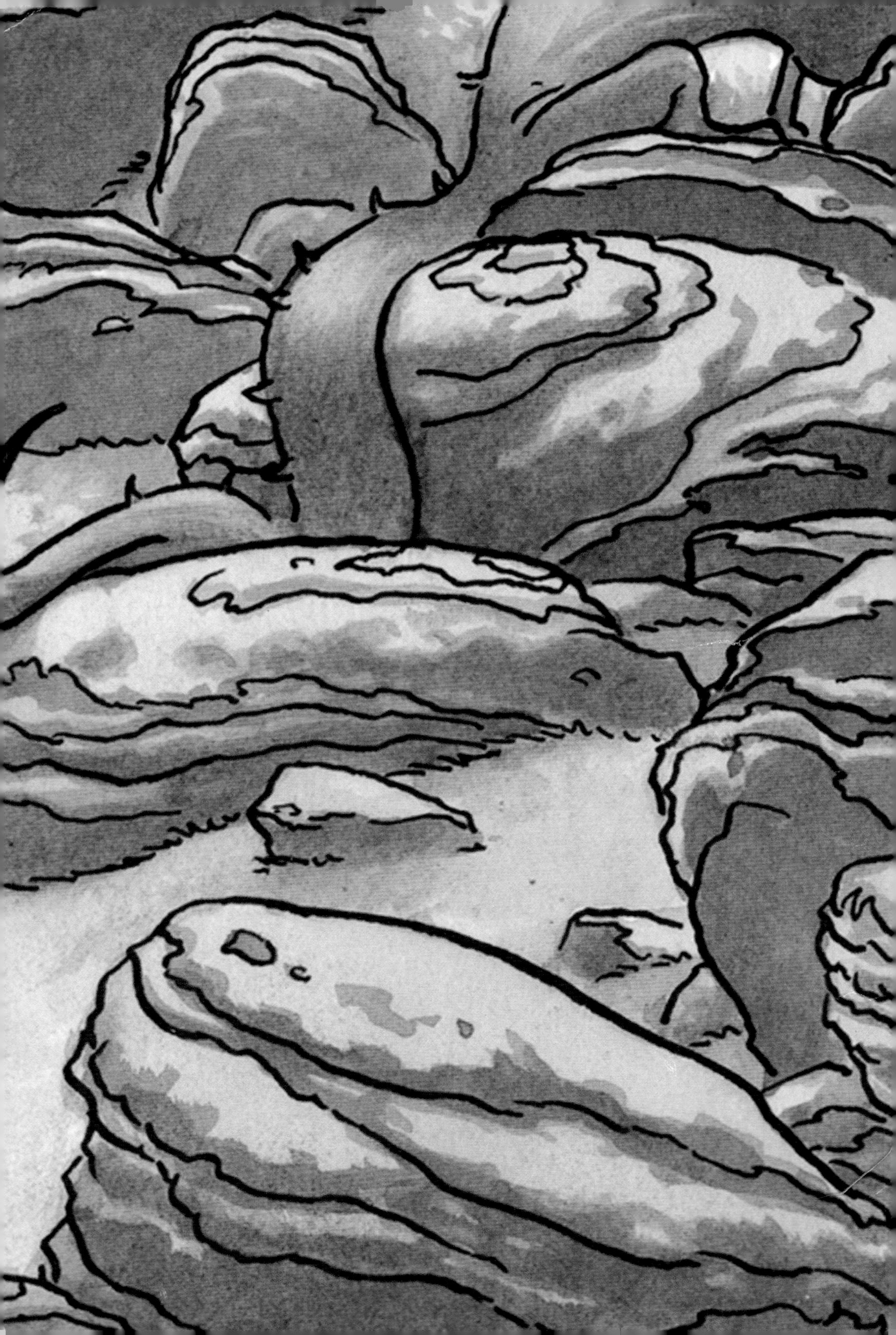

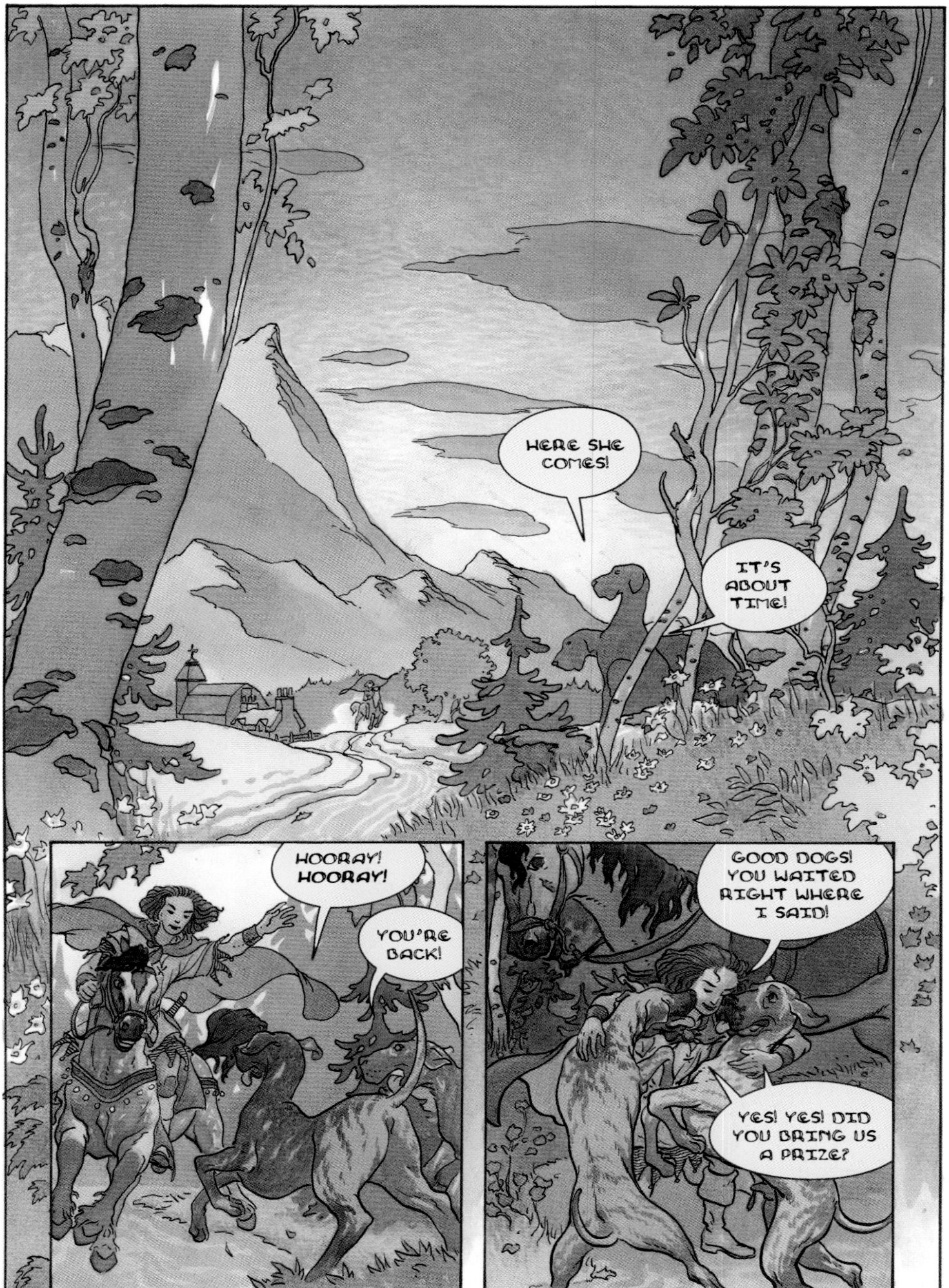
HERE SHE COMES!
IT'S ABOUT TIME!
HOORAY! HOORAY!
YOU'RE BACK!
GOOD DOGS! YOU WAITED RIGHT WHERE I SAID!
YES! YES! DID YOU BRING US A PRIZE?

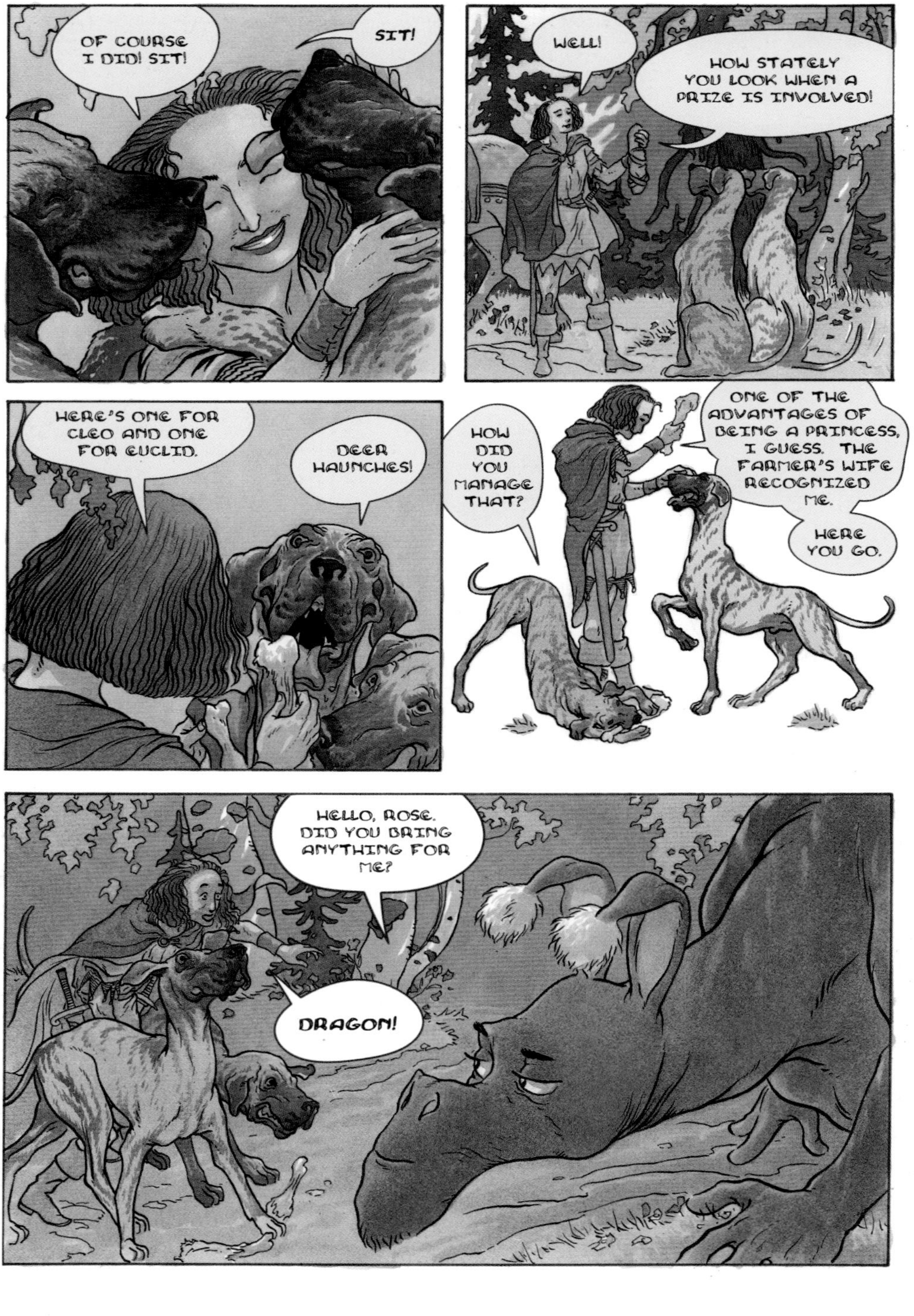
OF COURSE I DID! SIT!
SIT!
WELL!
HOW STATELY YOU LOOK WHEN A PRIZE IS INVOLVED!
HERE'S ONE FOR CLEO AND ONE FOR EUCLID.
DEER HAUNCHES!
HOW DID YOU MANAGE THAT?
ONE OF THE ADVANTAGES OF BEING A PRINCESS, I GUESS. THE FARMER'S WIFE RECOGNIZED ME.
HERE YOU GO.
HELLO, ROSE. DID YOU BRING ANYTHING FOR ME?
DRAGON!

I'M BEGINNING TO WONDER IF THE ICE QUEEN ISN'T RIGHT. WHY DID YOUR MOTHER AND FATHER SEND US ON THIS CRAZY ADVENTURE IN THE FIRST PLACE?

YES, BUT COULDN'T WE HAVE DONE IT IN ATHEIA INSTEAD OF THIS BACKWARD PLACE?

OLD MAN'S CAVE IS THE SANCTUARY OF THE DISCIPLES OF VENU. THIS IS WHERE I MUST PASS MY FINAL TEST!

BECAUSE AS A MEMBER OF THE ROYAL FAMILY, I MUST BE TRAINED TO LEAD THE DISCIPLES OF VENU AS WELL AS OUR PEOPLE.

HOLD IT! DID YOU SEE THAT?

LOOK AT THAT PERSON GOING INTO THE MOUNTAINS!

THAT LOOKS LIKE BRIAR! ISN'T SHE SUPPOSED TO BE IN YOUR CLASS WITH YOU?

I WONDER WHAT SHE'S UP TO?

SHE'S DEFINITELY NOT GOING TO CLASS. COME ON! LET'S FOLLOW HER!

ARE YOU SURE THAT'S A GOOD IDEA?

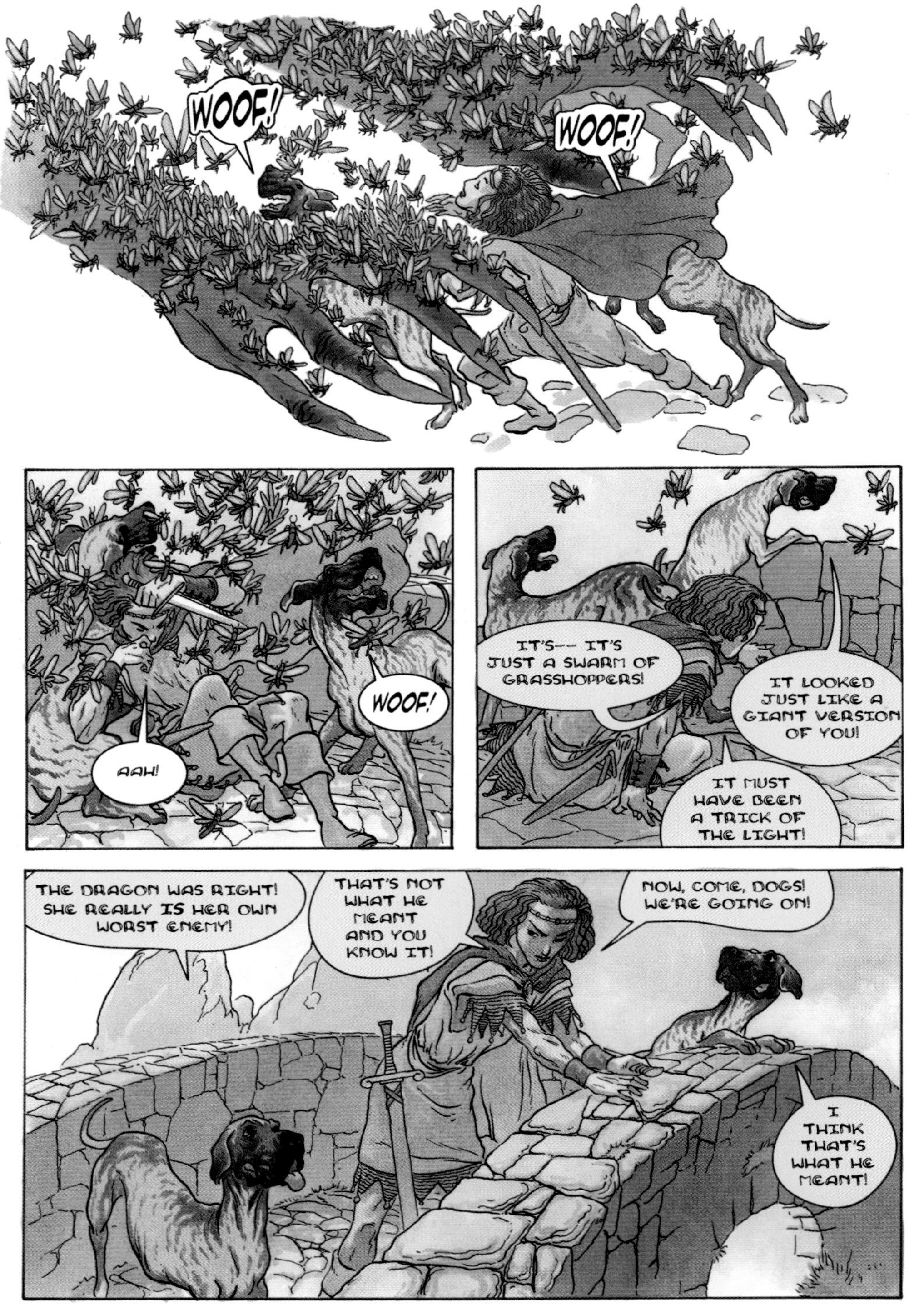
WOOF!
WOOF!
AAH!
WOOF!
IT'S-- IT'S JUST A SWARM OF GRASSHOPPERS!
IT LOOKED JUST LIKE A GIANT VERSION OF YOU!
IT MUST HAVE BEEN A TRICK OF THE LIGHT!
THE DRAGON WAS RIGHT! SHE REALLY IS HER OWN WORST ENEMY!
THAT'S NOT WHAT HE MEANT AND YOU KNOW IT!
NOW, COME, DOGS! WE'RE GOING ON!
I THINK THAT'S WHAT HE MEANT!

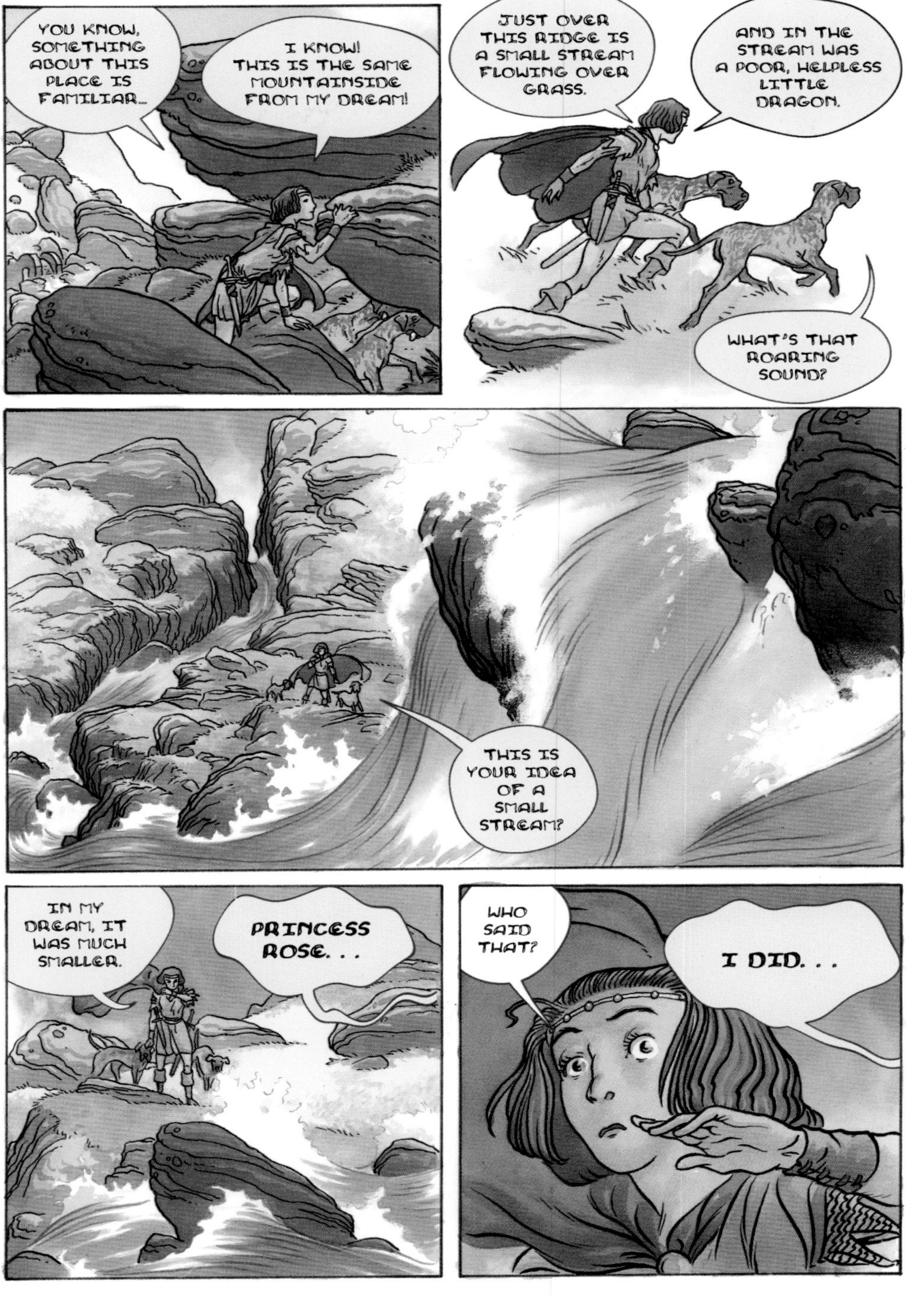
YOU KNOW, SOMETHING ABOUT THIS PLACE IS FAMILIAR...
I KNOW! THIS IS THE SAME MOUNTAINSIDE FROM MY DREAM!
JUST OVER THIS RIDGE IS A SMALL STREAM FLOWING OVER GRASS.
AND IN THE STREAM WAS A POOR, HELPLESS LITTLE DRAGON.
WHAT'S THAT ROARING SOUND?
THIS IS YOUR IDEA OF A SMALL STREAM?
IN MY DREAM, IT WAS MUCH SMALLER.
PRINCESS ROSE. . .
WHO SAID THAT?
I DID. . .

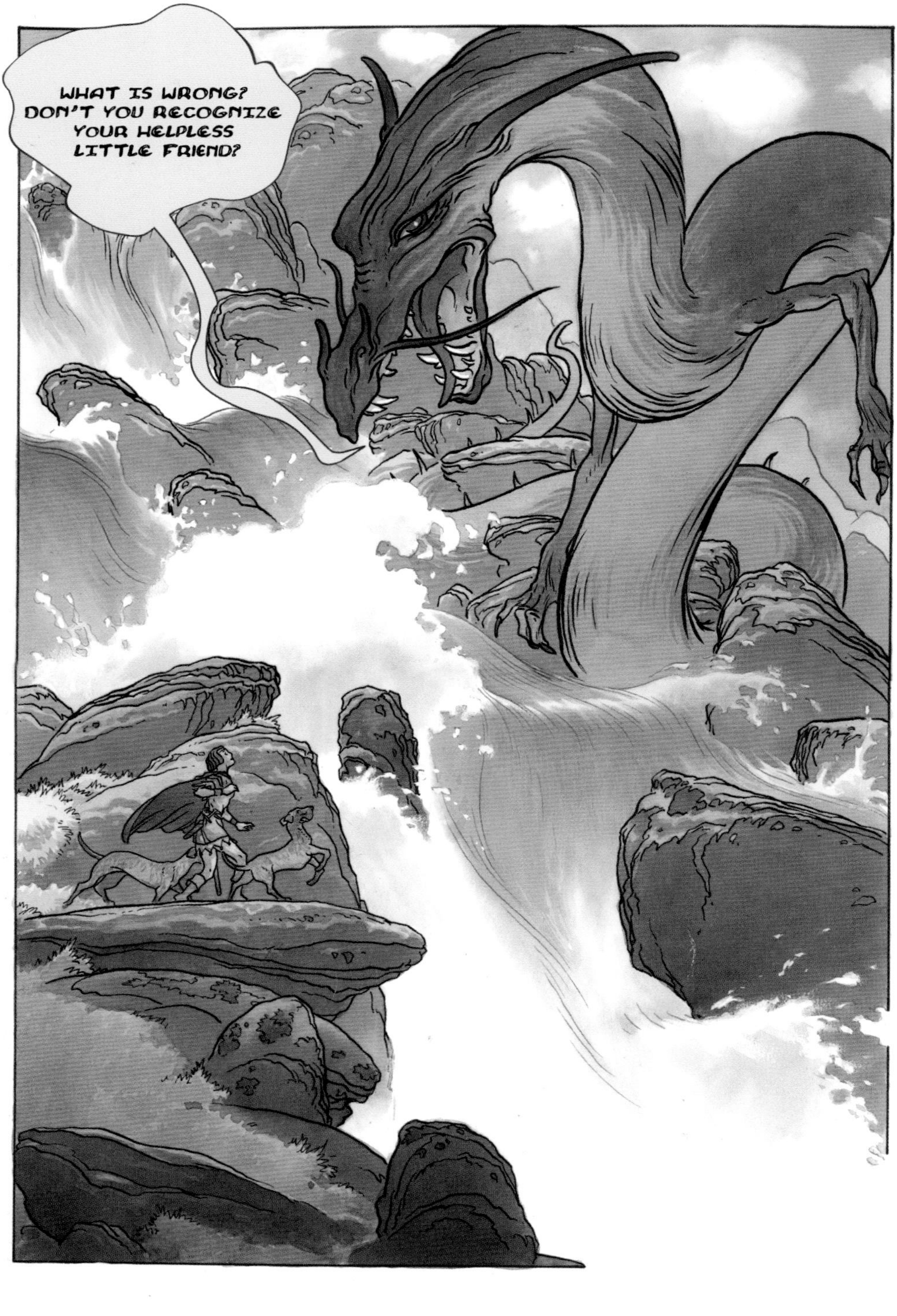
WHAT IS WRONG? DON'T YOU RECOGNIZE YOUR HELPLESS LITTLE FRIEND?

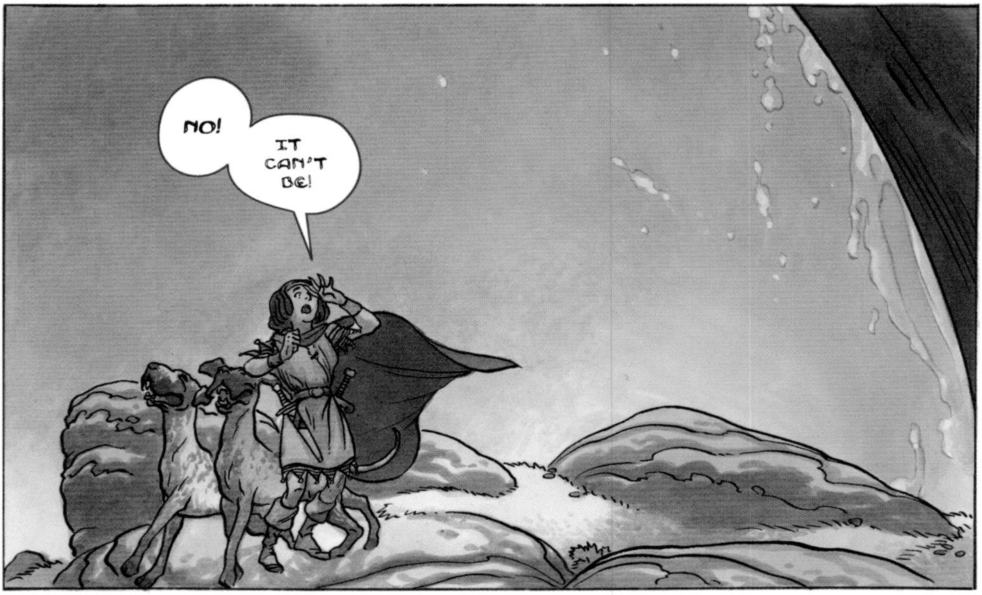
NO!
IT CAN'T BE!

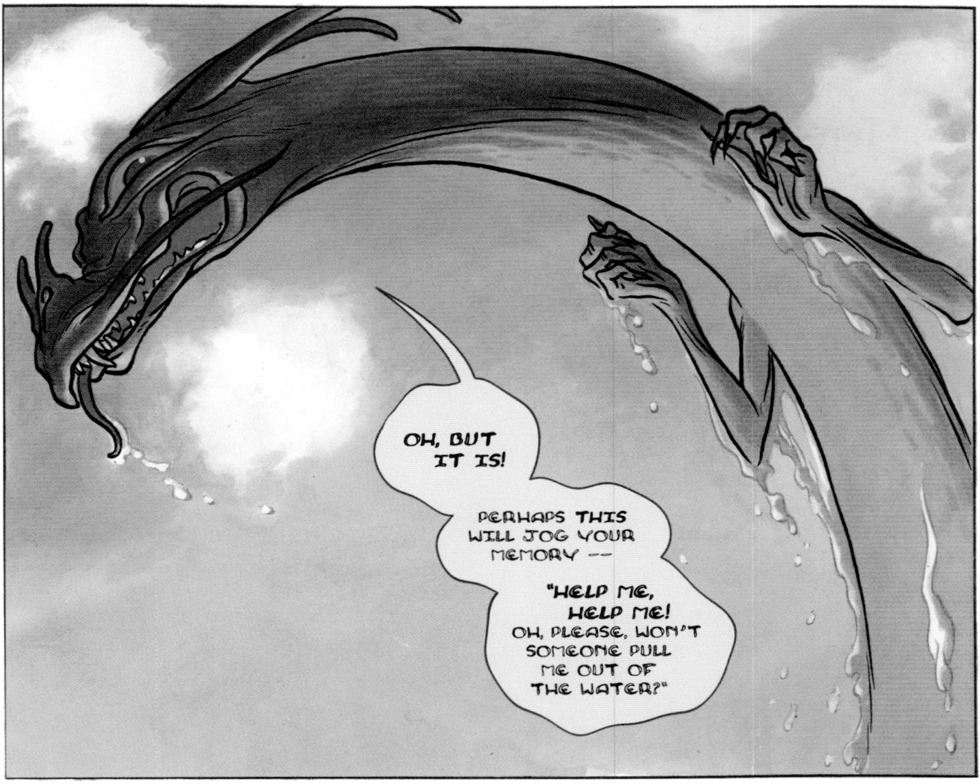
OH, BUT IT IS!
PERHAPS THIS WILL JOG YOUR MEMORY --
"HELP ME, HELP ME! OH, PLEASE, WON'T SOMEONE PULL ME OUT OF THE WATER?"

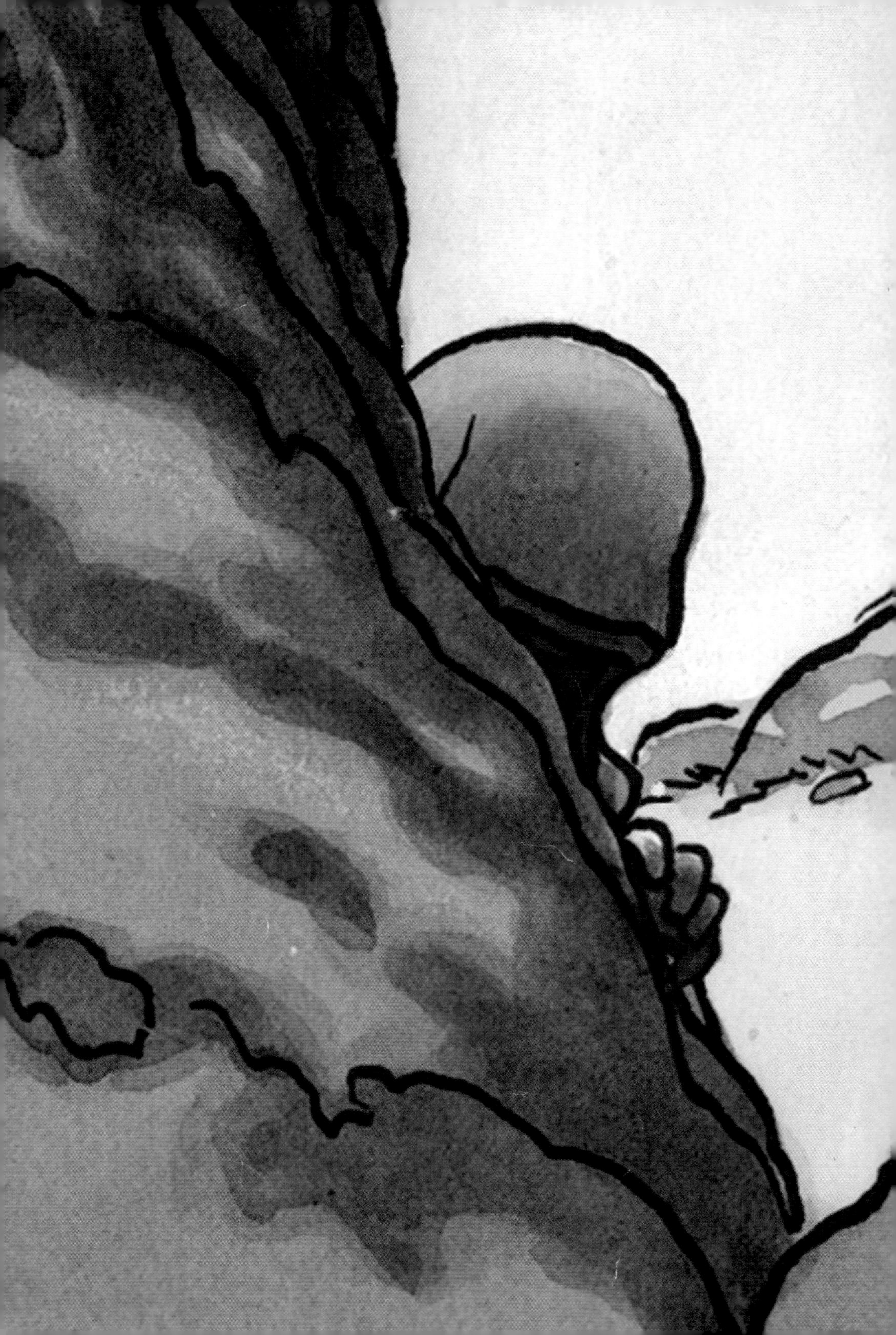

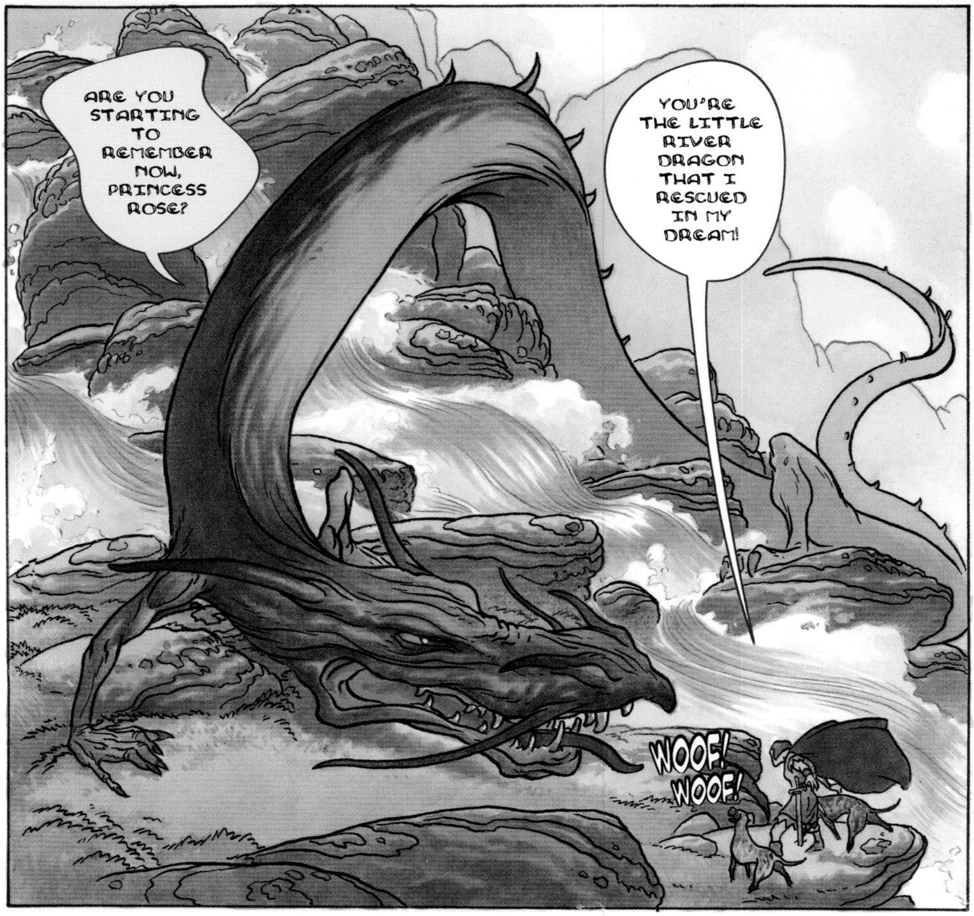
ARE YOU STARTING TO REMEMBER NOW, PRINCESS ROSE?
YOU'RE THE LITTLE RIVER DRAGON THAT I RESCUED IN MY DREAM!
WOOF! WOOF!

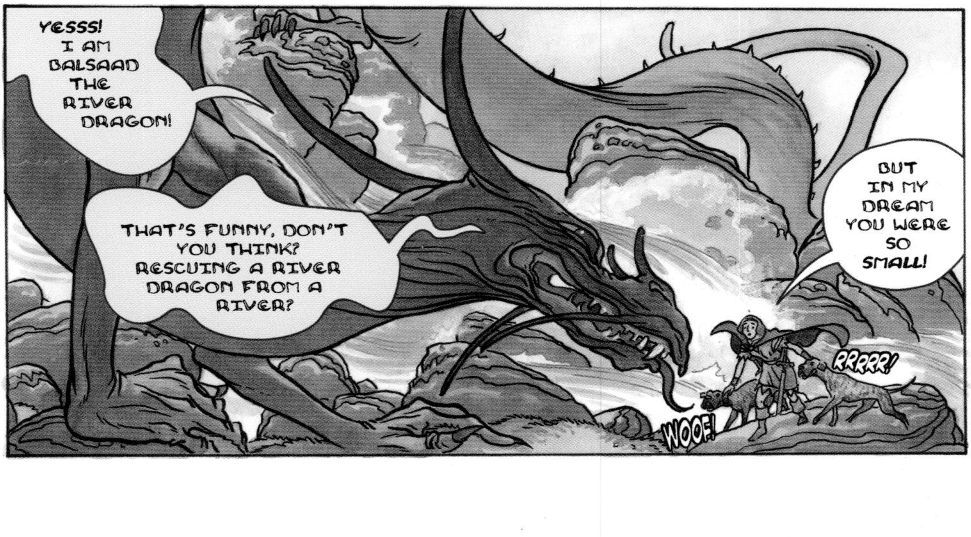
YESSS! I AM BALSAAD THE RIVER DRAGON!
THAT'S FUNNY, DON'T YOU THINK? RESCUING A RIVER DRAGON FROM A RIVER?
BUT IN MY DREAM YOU WERE SO SMALL!
RRRRR!
WOOF!

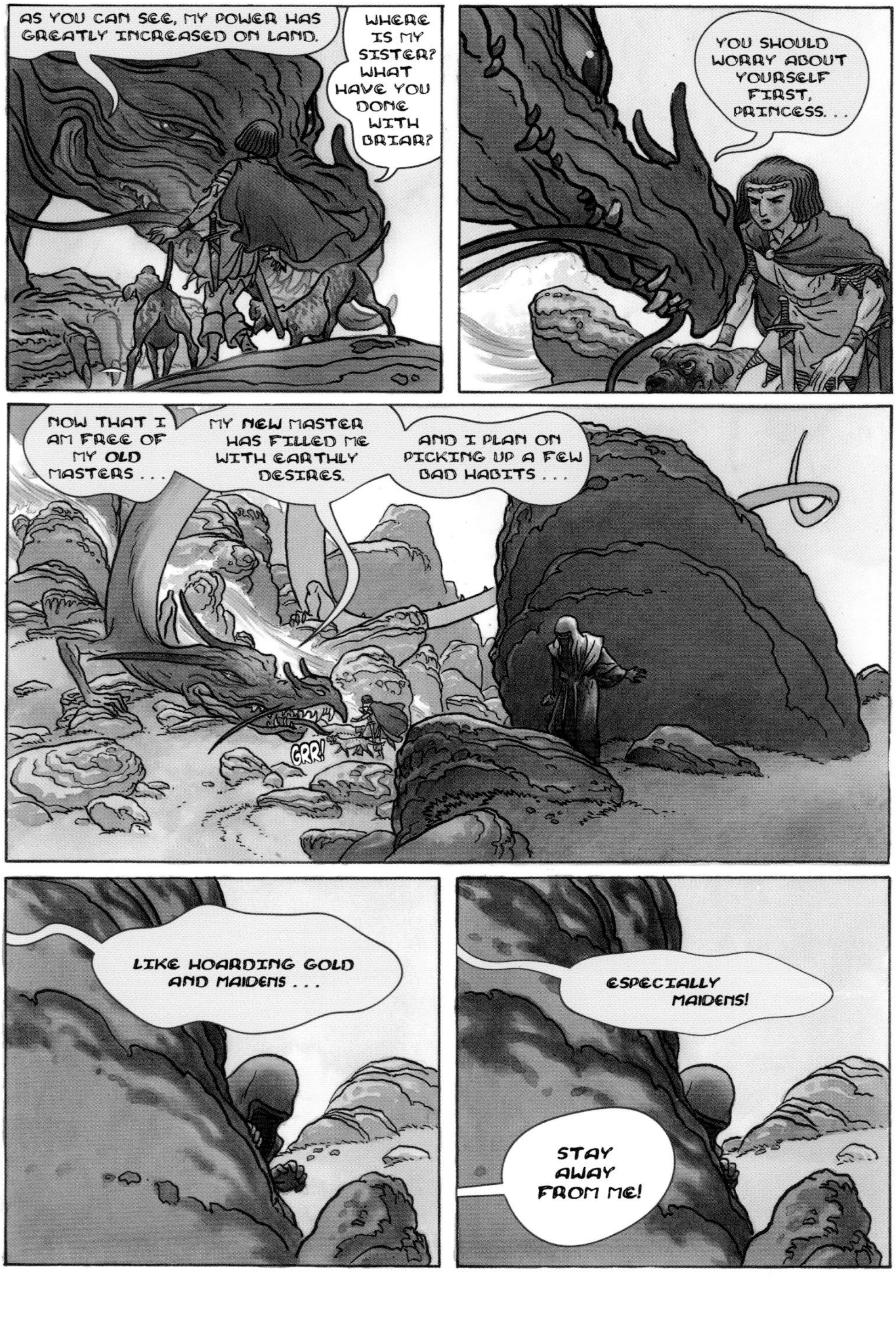
AS YOU CAN SEE, MY POWER HAS GREATLY INCREASED ON LAND.
WHERE IS MY SISTER? WHAT HAVE YOU DONE WITH BRIAR?
YOU SHOULD WORRY ABOUT YOURSELF FIRST, PRINCESS. . .
NOW THAT I AM FREE OF MY OLD MASTERS . . .
MY NEW MASTER HAS FILLED ME WITH EARTHLY DESIRES.
AND I PLAN ON PICKING UP A FEW BAD HABITS . . .
GRR!
LIKE HOARDING GOLD AND MAIDENS . . .
ESPECIALLY MAIDENS!
STAY AWAY FROM ME!

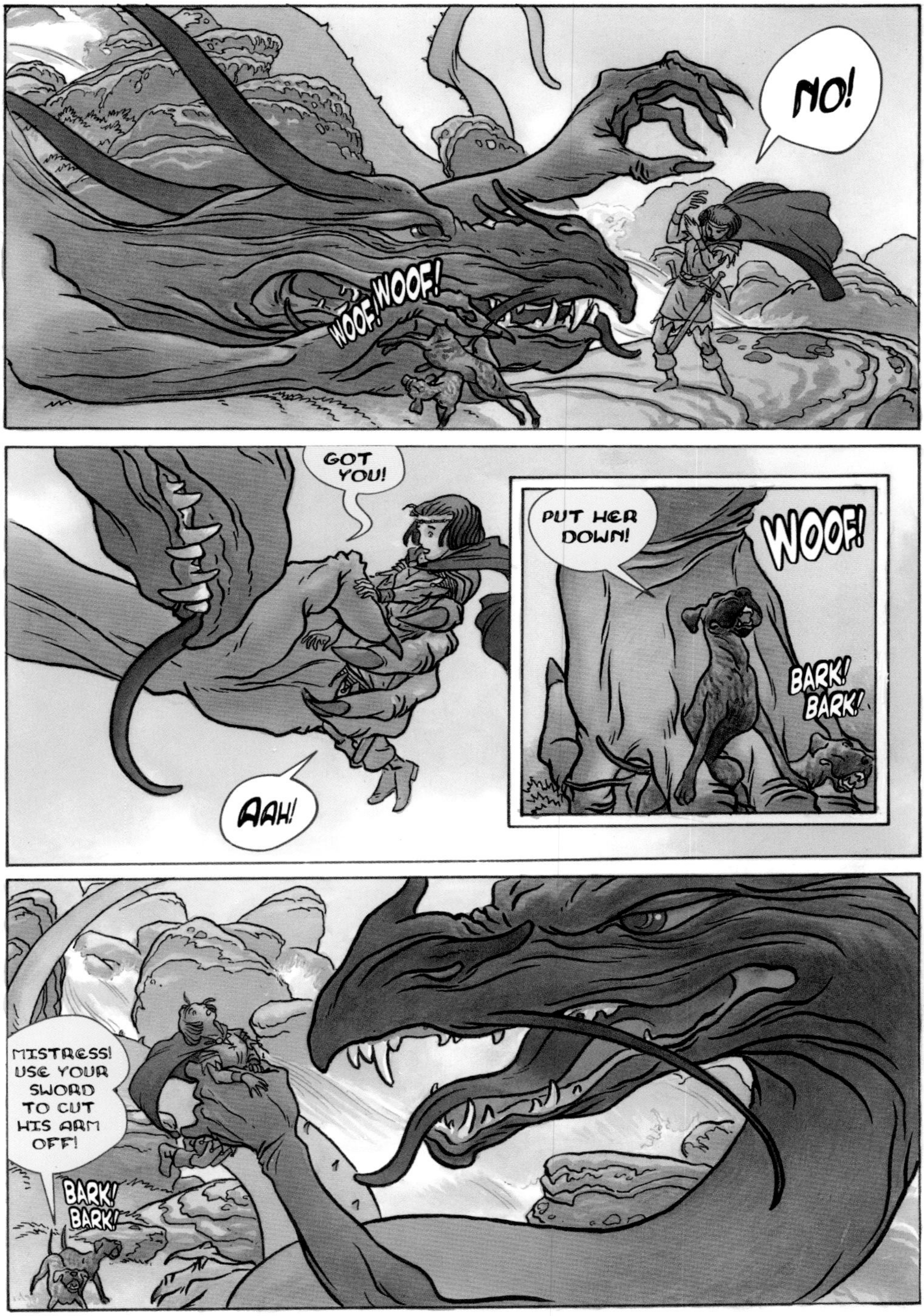
NO!
WOOF! WOOF!
GOT YOU!
AAH!
PUT HER DOWN!
WOOF!
BARK! BARK!
MISTRESS! USE YOUR SWORD TO CUT HIS ARM OFF!
BARK! BARK!

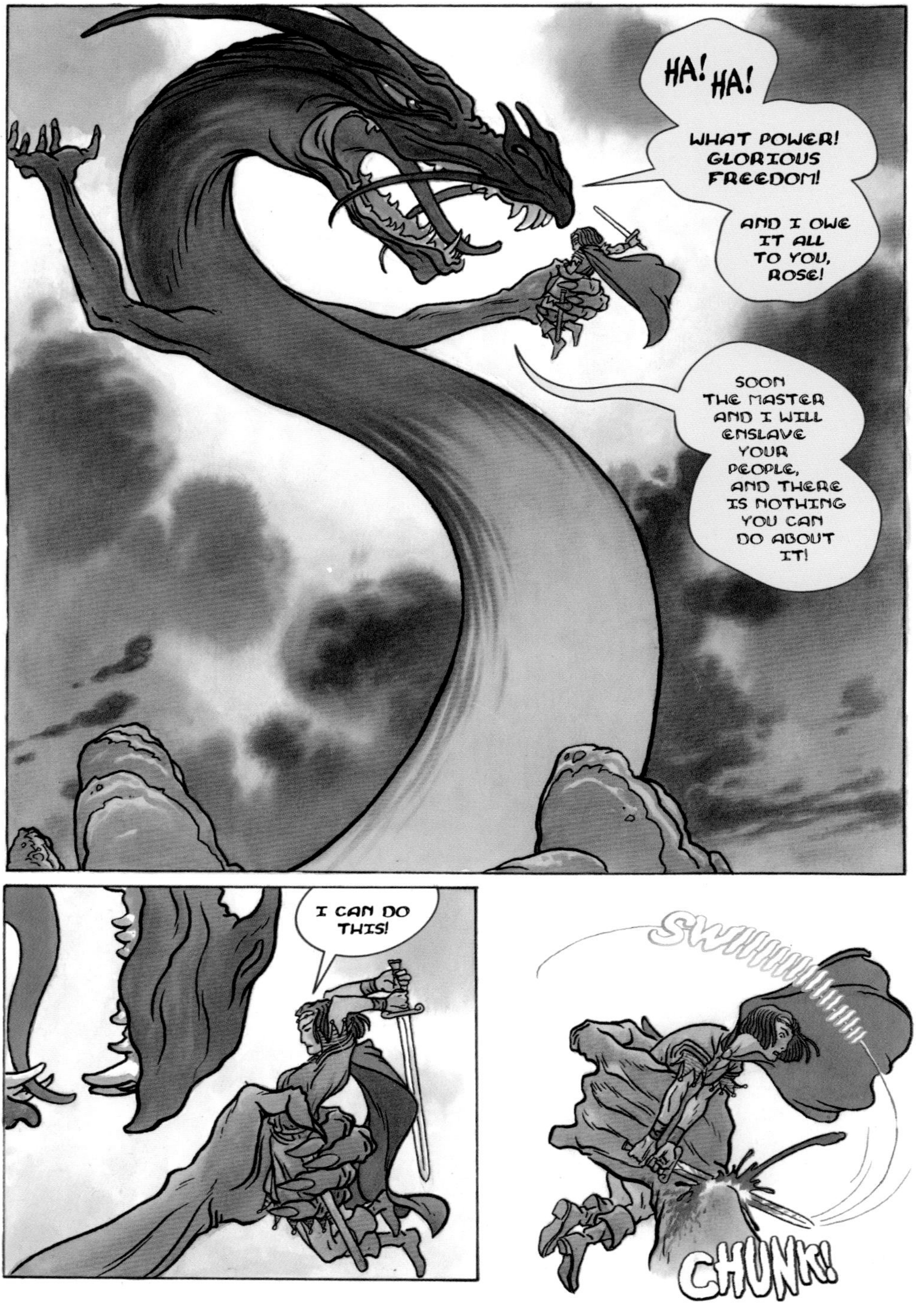
HA! HA!
WHAT POWER! GLORIOUS FREEDOM!
AND I OWE IT ALL TO YOU, ROSE!
SOON THE MASTER AND I WILL ENSLAVE YOUR PEOPLE, AND THERE IS NOTHING YOU CAN DO ABOUT IT!
I CAN DO THIS!
SWIIIIIIII
CHUNK!

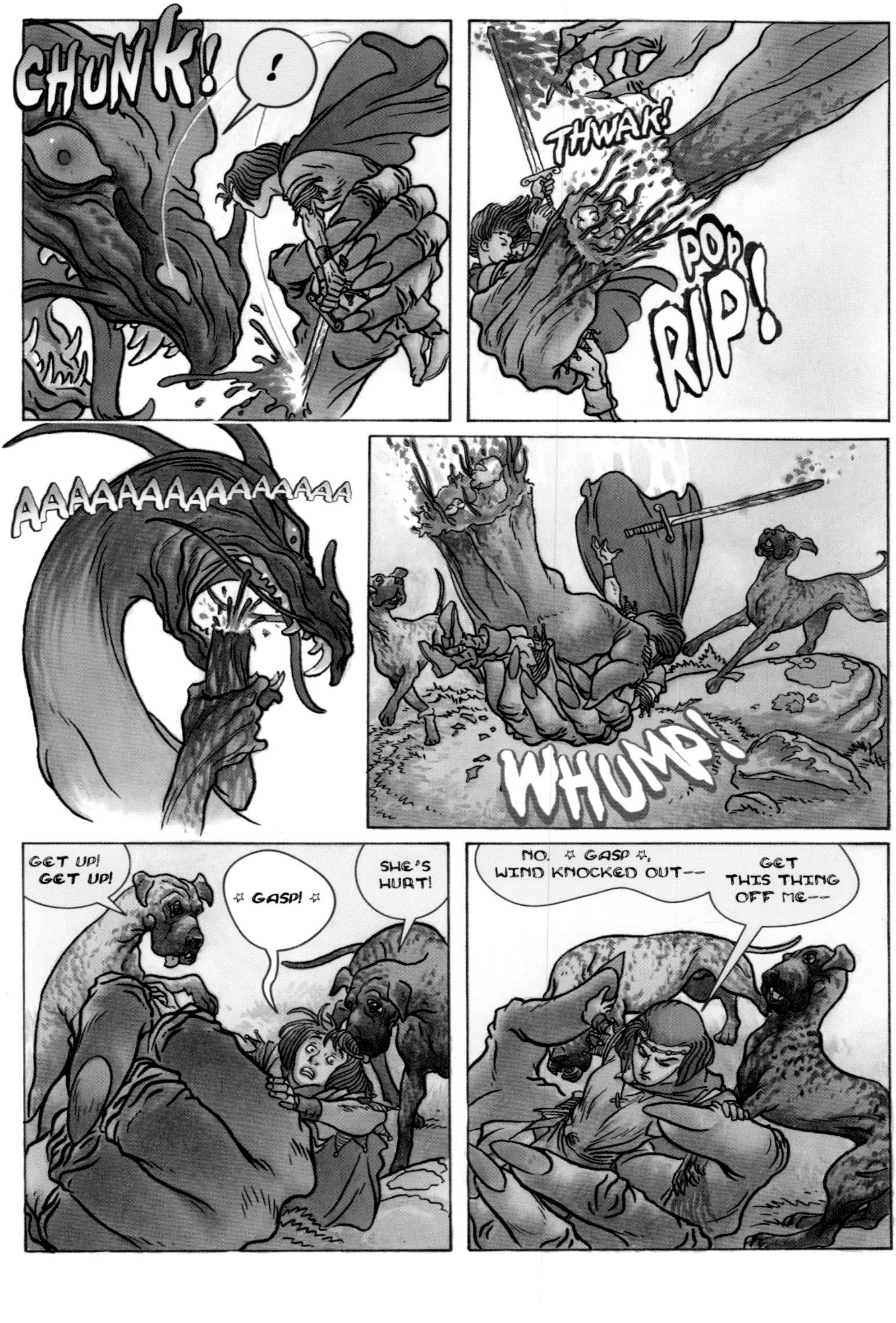
CHUNK!
!
THWAK!
POP
RIP!
AAAAAAAAAAAAAAA
WHUMP!
GET UP! GET UP!
☆ GASP! ☆
SHE'S HURT!
NO. ☆ GASP ☆, WIND KNOCKED OUT--
GET THIS THING OFF ME--

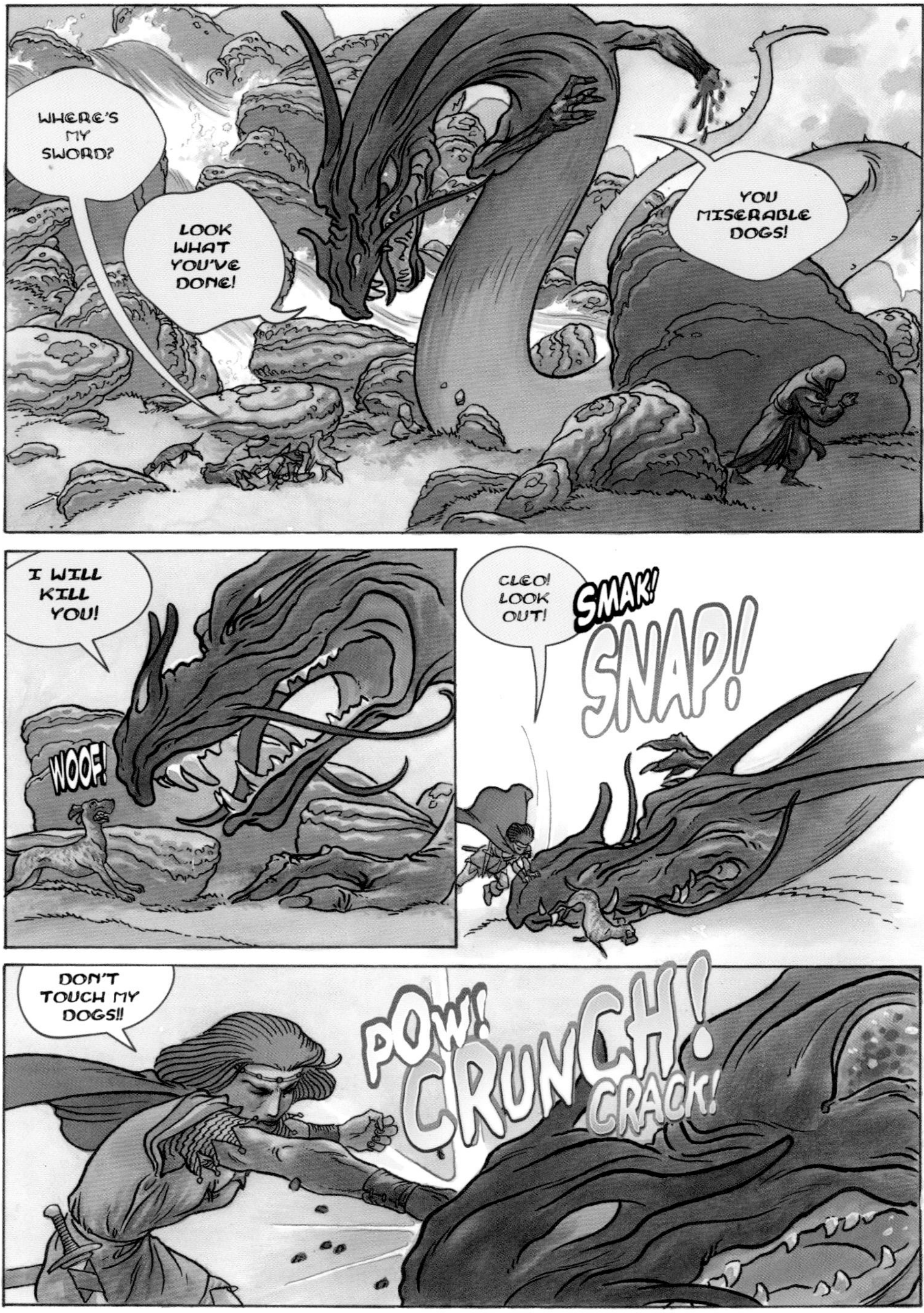
WHERE'S MY SWORD?
LOOK WHAT YOU'VE DONE!
YOU MISERABLE DOGS!
I WILL KILL YOU!
WOOF!
CLEO! LOOK OUT!
SMAK!
SNAP!
DON'T TOUCH MY DOGS!!
POW!
CRUNCH!
CRACK!

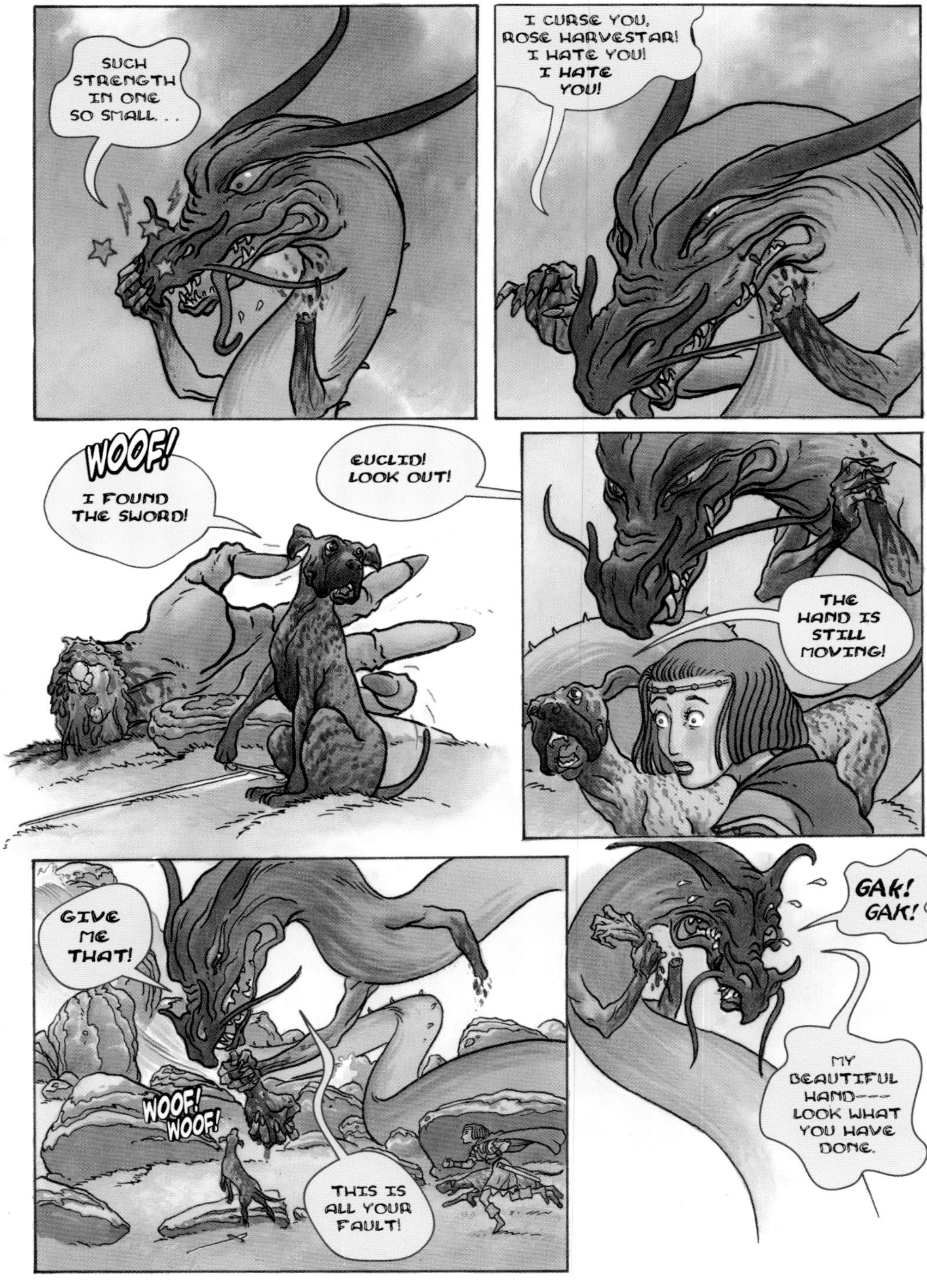
SUCH STRENGTH IN ONE SO SMALL. . .
I CURSE YOU, ROSE HARVESTAR! I HATE YOU! I HATE YOU!
WOOF!
I FOUND THE SWORD!
EUCLID! LOOK OUT!
THE HAND IS STILL MOVING!
GIVE ME THAT!
WOOF! WOOF!
THIS IS ALL YOUR FAULT!
GAK! GAK!
MY BEAUTIFUL HAND--- LOOK WHAT YOU HAVE DONE.

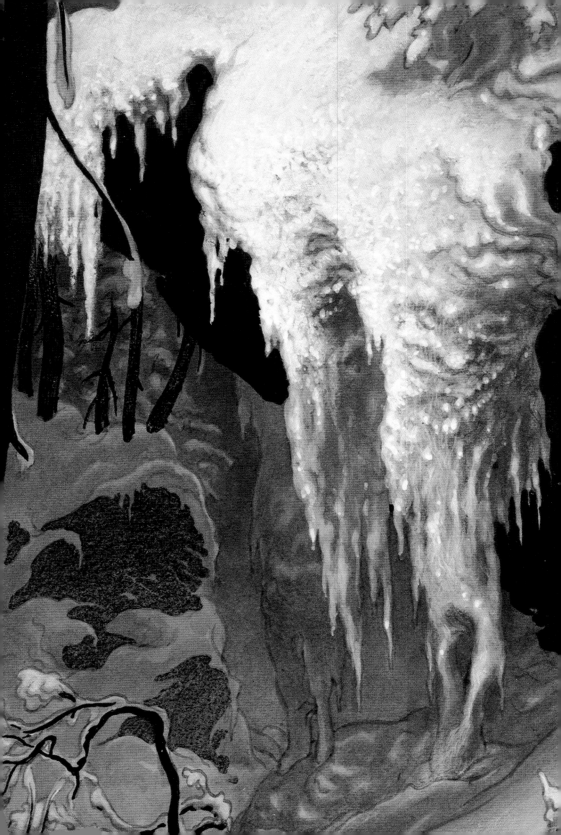

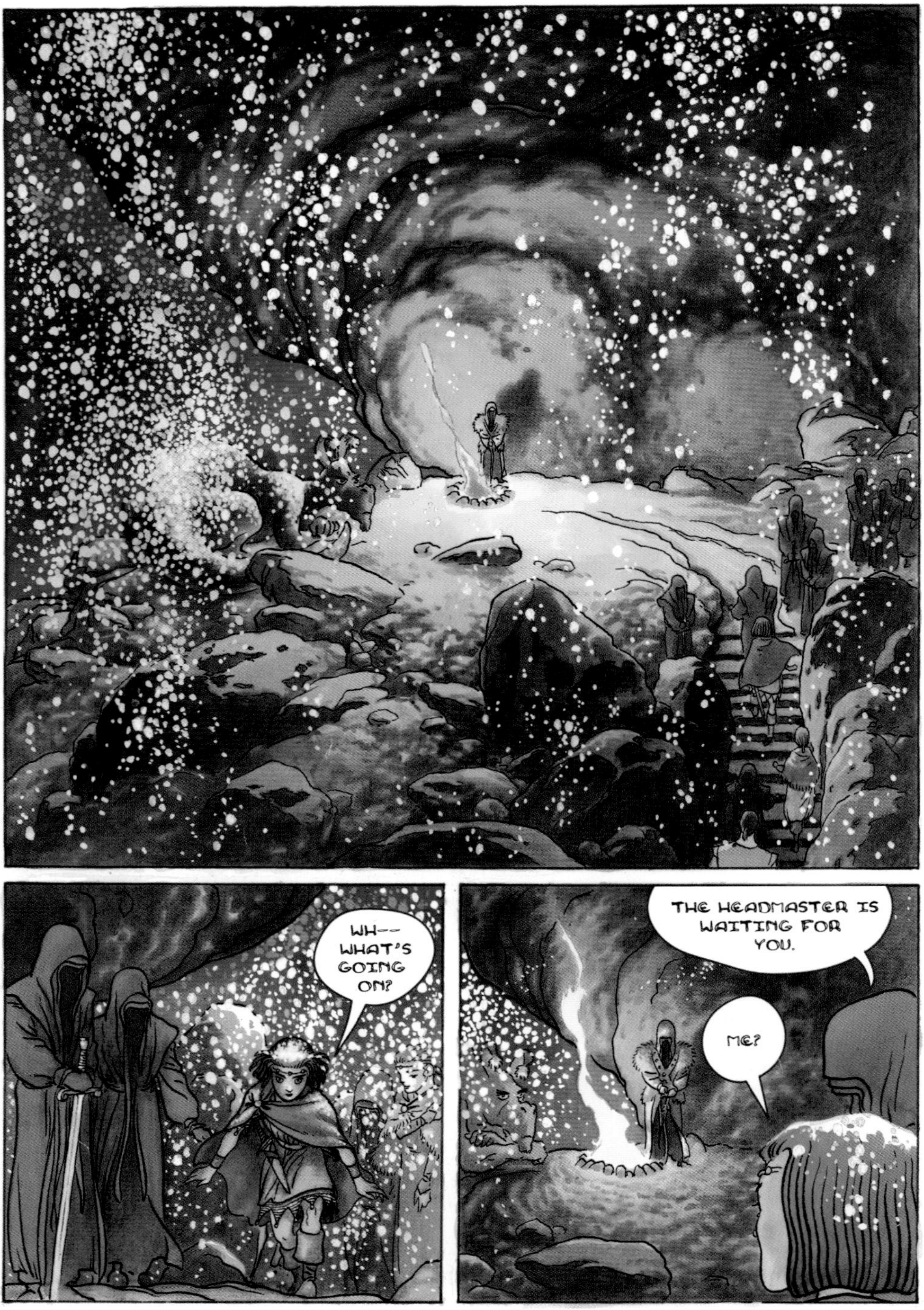
WH--
WHAT'S GOING ON?
THE HEADMASTER IS WAITING FOR YOU.
ME?

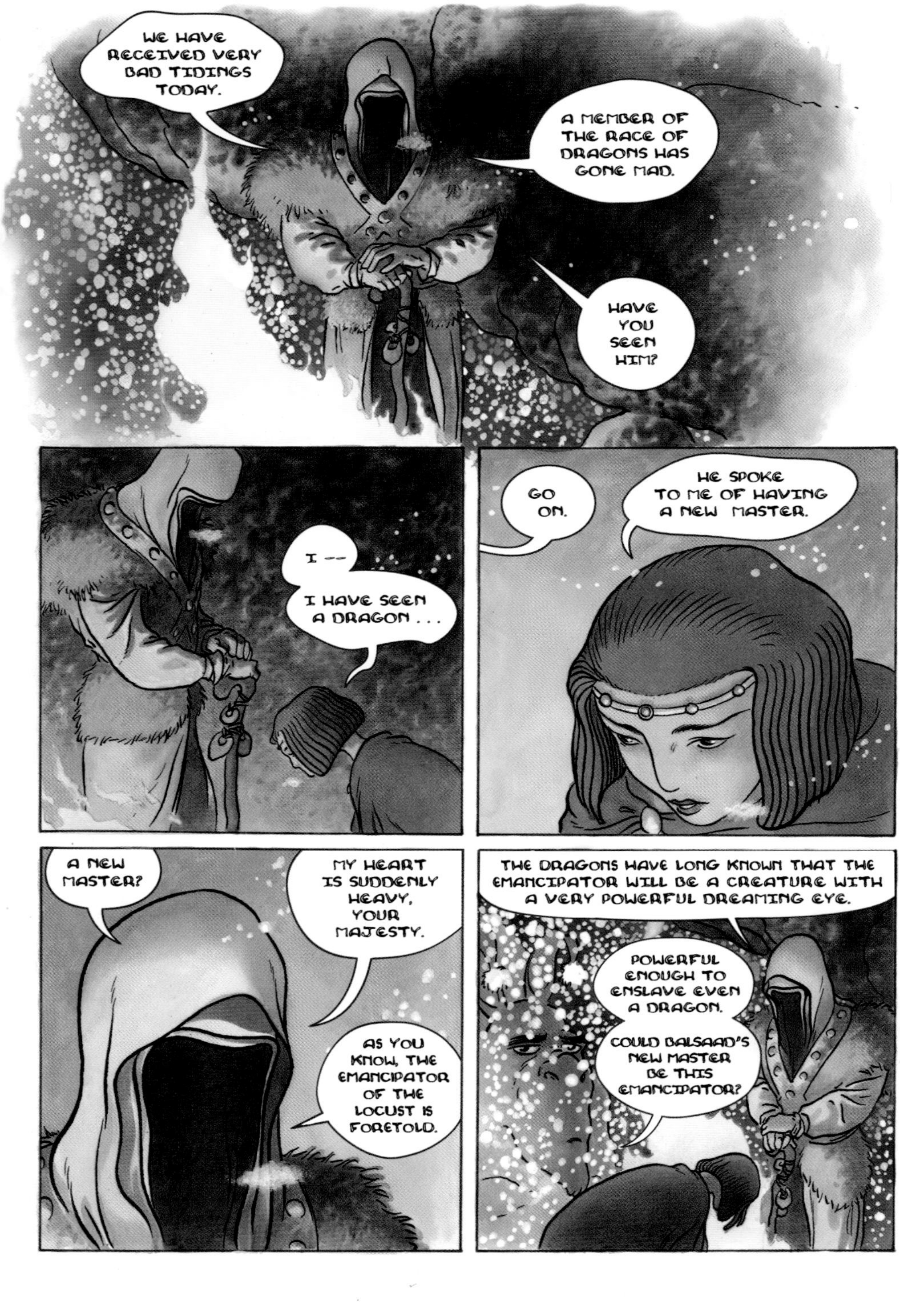
WE HAVE RECEIVED VERY BAD TIDINGS TODAY.
A MEMBER OF THE RACE OF DRAGONS HAS GONE MAD.
HAVE YOU SEEN HIM?
I --
I HAVE SEEN A DRAGON . . .
GO ON.
HE SPOKE TO ME OF HAVING A NEW MASTER.
A NEW MASTER?
MY HEART IS SUDDENLY HEAVY, YOUR MAJESTY.
AS YOU KNOW, THE EMANCIPATOR OF THE LOCUST IS FORETOLD.
THE DRAGONS HAVE LONG KNOWN THAT THE EMANCIPATOR WILL BE A CREATURE WITH A VERY POWERFUL DREAMING EYE.
POWERFUL ENOUGH TO ENSLAVE EVEN A DRAGON.
COULD BALSAAD'S NEW MASTER BE THIS EMANCIPATOR?

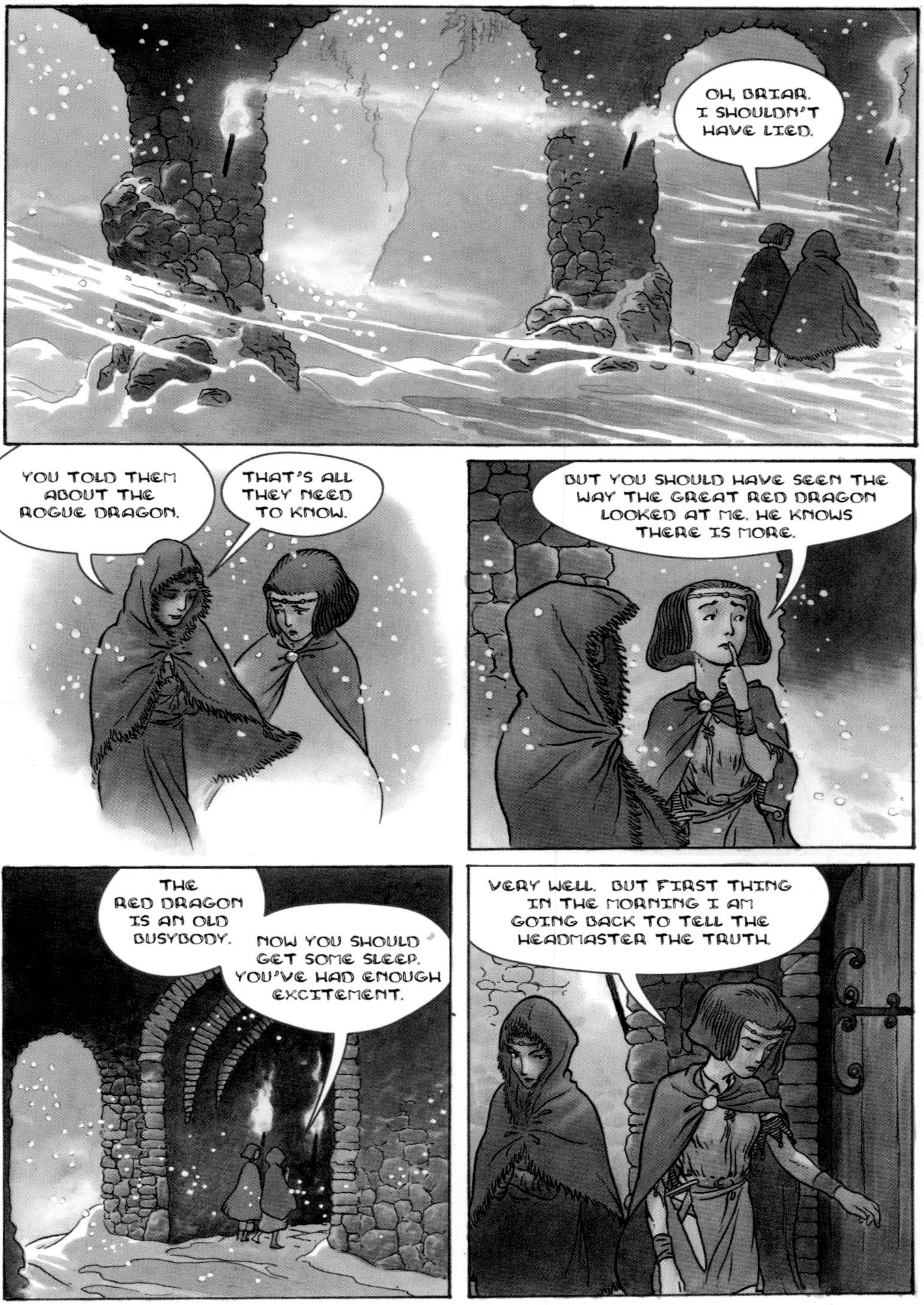
OH, BRIAR. I SHOULDN'T HAVE LIED.
YOU TOLD THEM ABOUT THE ROGUE DRAGON.
THAT'S ALL THEY NEED TO KNOW.
BUT YOU SHOULD HAVE SEEN THE WAY THE GREAT RED DRAGON LOOKED AT ME. HE KNOWS THERE IS MORE.
THE RED DRAGON IS AN OLD BUSYBODY.
NOW YOU SHOULD GET SOME SLEEP. YOU'VE HAD ENOUGH EXCITEMENT.
VERY WELL. BUT FIRST THING IN THE MORNING I AM GOING BACK TO TELL THE HEADMASTER THE TRUTH.

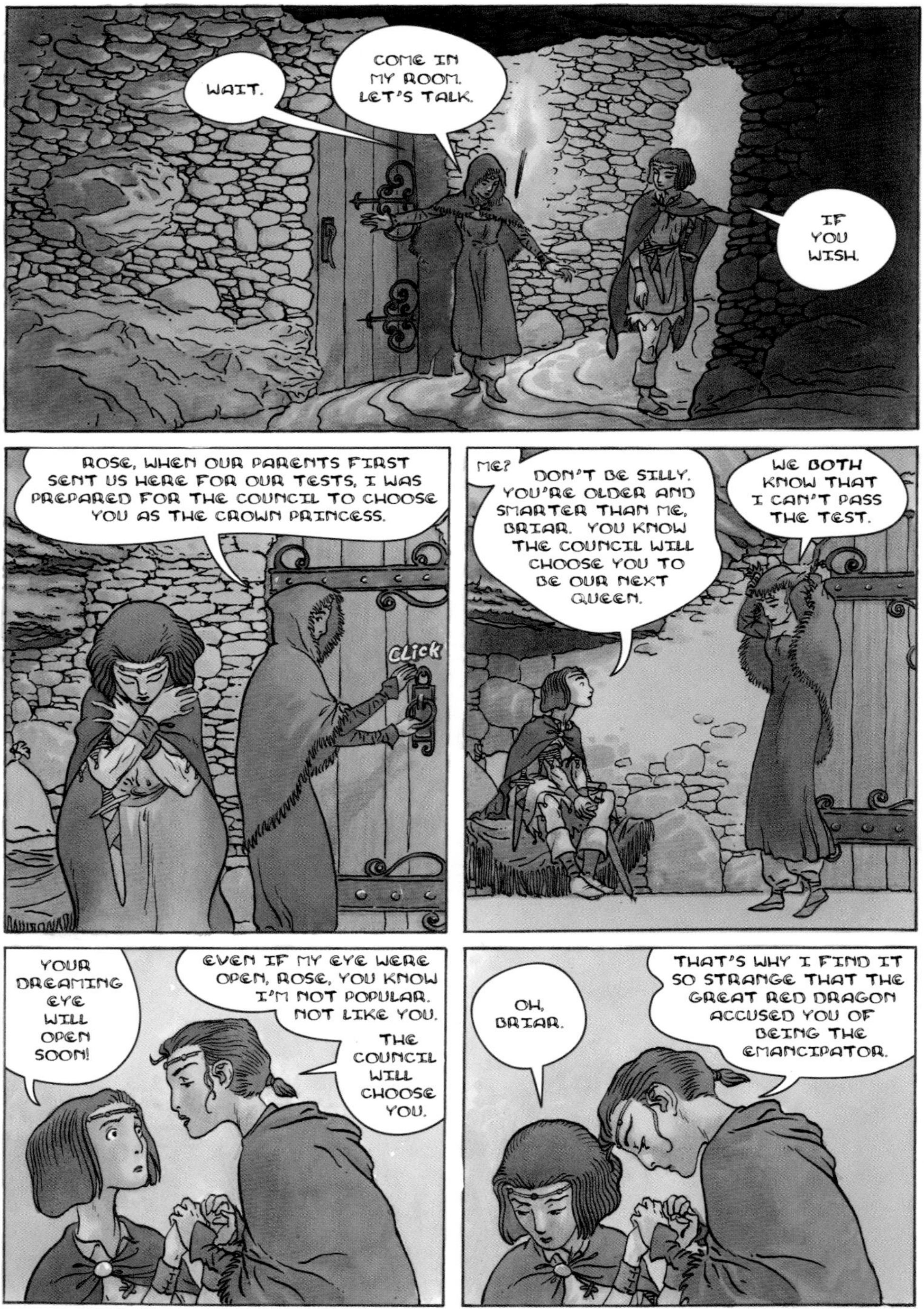
WAIT.
COME IN MY ROOM. LET'S TALK.
IF YOU WISH.
ROSE, WHEN OUR PARENTS FIRST SENT US HERE FOR OUR TESTS, I WAS PREPARED FOR THE COUNCIL TO CHOOSE YOU AS THE CROWN PRINCESS.
CLICK
ME?
DON'T BE SILLY. YOU'RE OLDER AND SMARTER THAN ME, BRIAR. YOU KNOW THE COUNCIL WILL CHOOSE YOU TO BE OUR NEXT QUEEN.
WE BOTH KNOW THAT I CAN'T PASS THE TEST.
YOUR DREAMING EYE WILL OPEN SOON!
EVEN IF MY EYE WERE OPEN, ROSE, YOU KNOW I'M NOT POPULAR. NOT LIKE YOU.
THE COUNCIL WILL CHOOSE YOU.
OH, BRIAR.
THAT'S WHY I FIND IT SO STRANGE THAT THE GREAT RED DRAGON ACCUSED YOU OF BEING THE EMANCIPATOR.

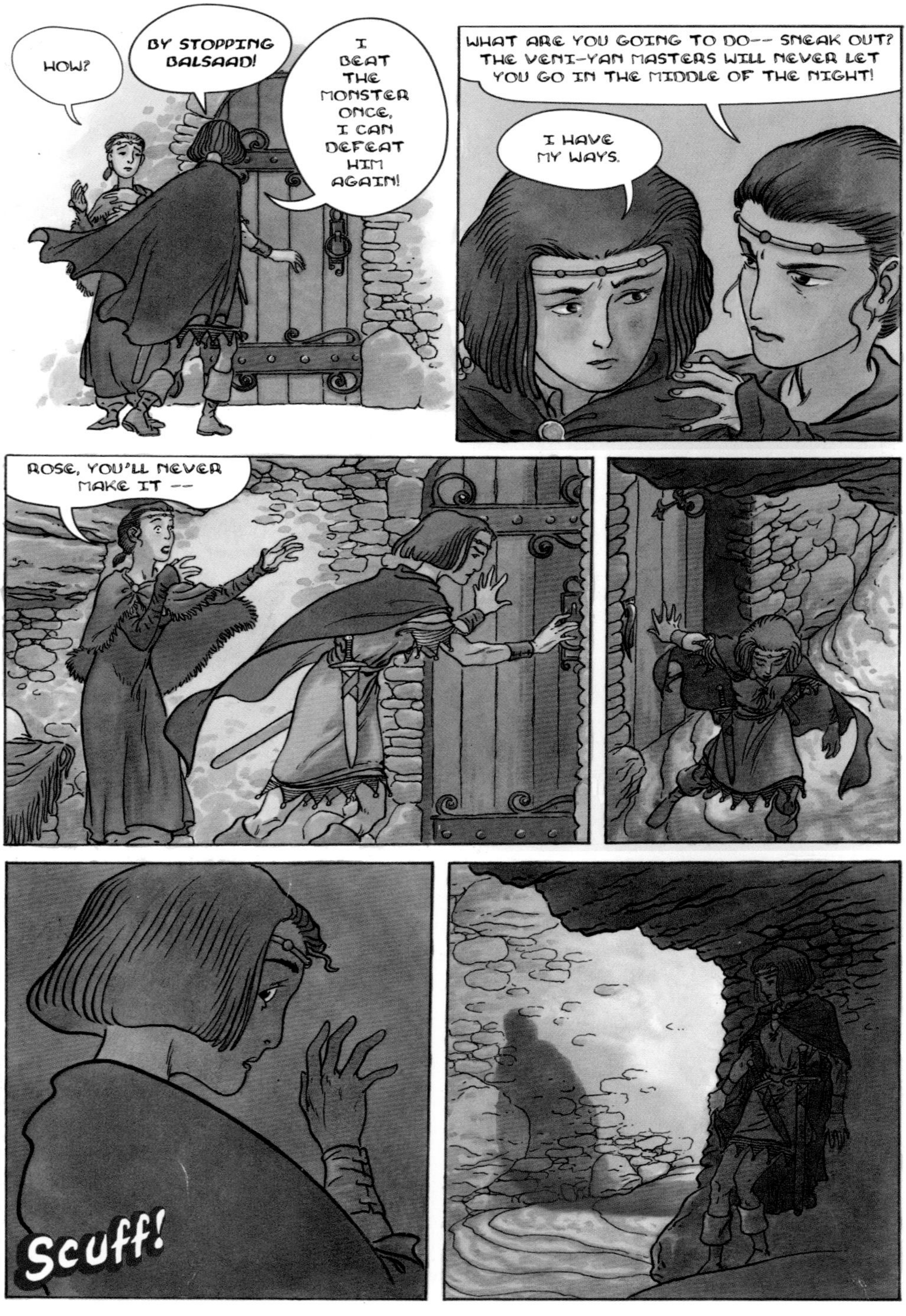
HOW?
BY STOPPING BALSAAD!
I BEAT THE MONSTER ONCE, I CAN DEFEAT HIM AGAIN!
WHAT ARE YOU GOING TO DO-- SNEAK OUT? THE VENI-YAN MASTERS WILL NEVER LET YOU GO IN THE MIDDLE OF THE NIGHT!
I HAVE MY WAYS.
ROSE, YOU'LL NEVER MAKE IT --
Scuff!

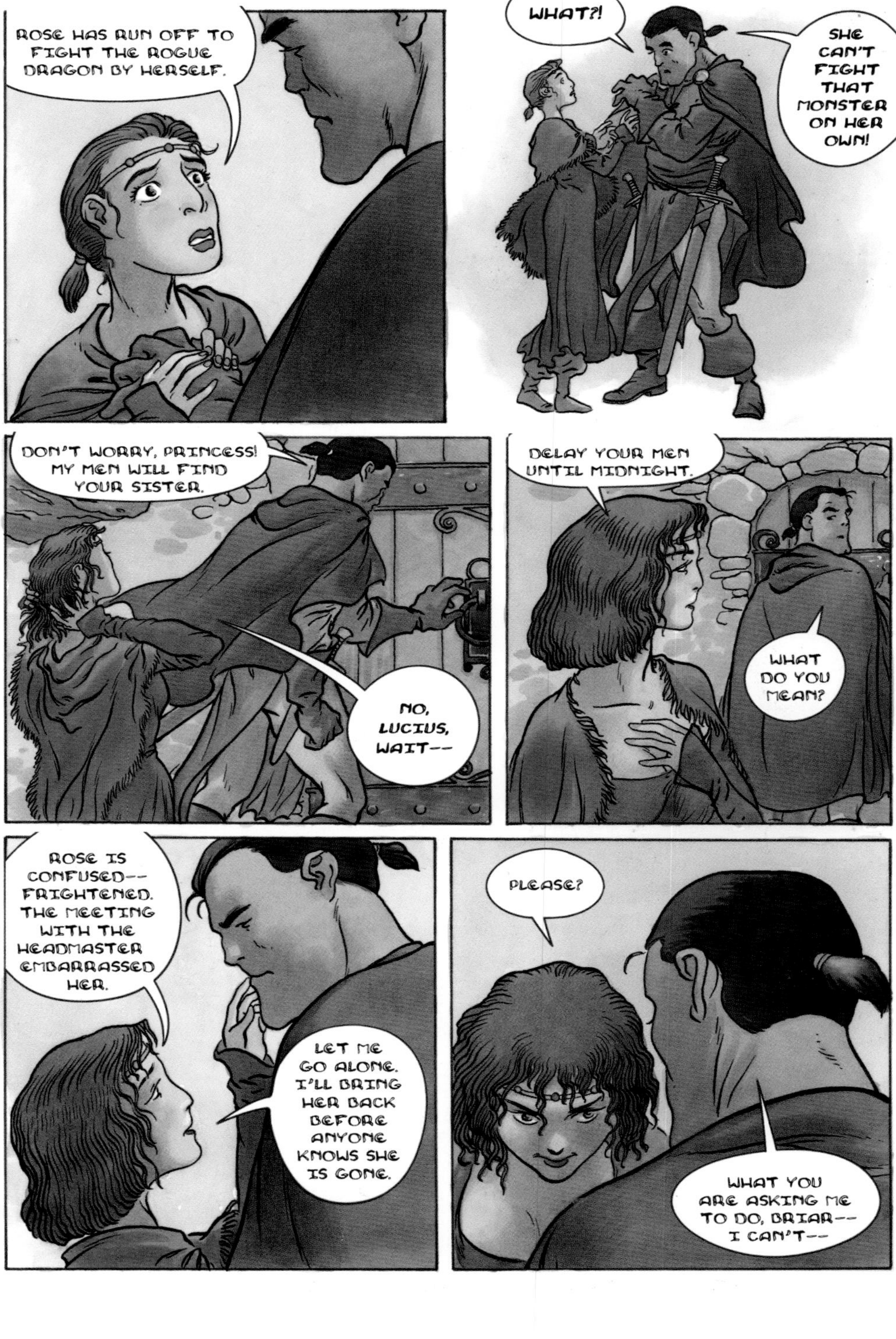
ROSE HAS RUN OFF TO FIGHT THE ROGUE DRAGON BY HERSELF.
WHAT?!
SHE CAN'T FIGHT THAT MONSTER ON HER OWN!
DON'T WORRY, PRINCESS! MY MEN WILL FIND YOUR SISTER.
NO, LUCIUS, WAIT--
DELAY YOUR MEN UNTIL MIDNIGHT.
WHAT DO YOU MEAN?
ROSE IS CONFUSED-- FRIGHTENED. THE MEETING WITH THE HEADMASTER EMBARRASSED HER.
LET ME GO ALONE. I'LL BRING HER BACK BEFORE ANYONE KNOWS SHE IS GONE.
PLEASE?
WHAT YOU ARE ASKING ME TO DO, BRIAR-- I CAN'T--

INTO THE NIGHT...

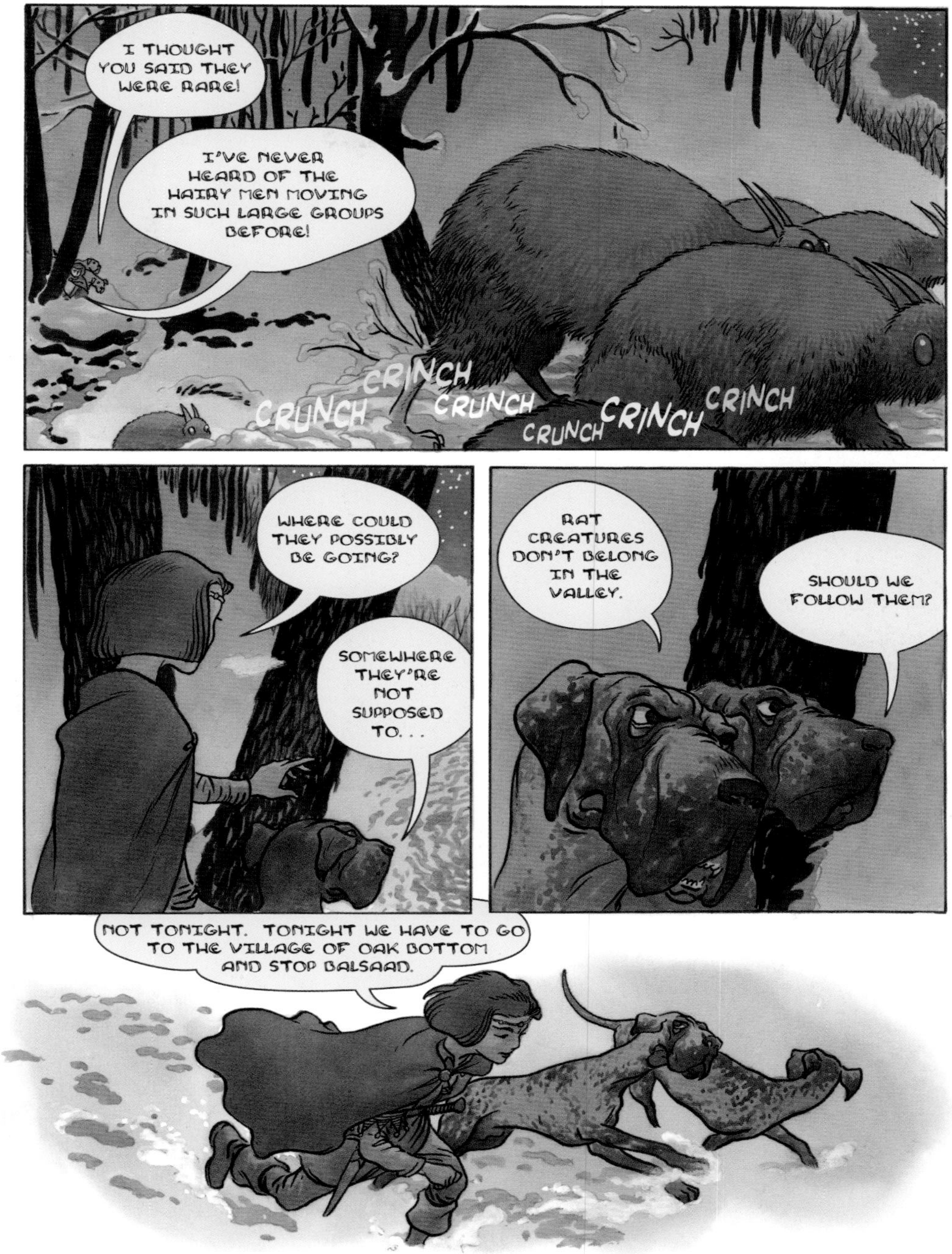
I THOUGHT YOU SAID THEY WERE RARE!
I'VE NEVER HEARD OF THE HAIRY MEN MOVING IN SUCH LARGE GROUPS BEFORE!
CRUNCH
CRINCH
CRUNCH
CRUNCH
CRINCH
CRINCH
WHERE COULD THEY POSSIBLY BE GOING?
SOMEWHERE THEY'RE NOT SUPPOSED TO. . .
RAT CREATURES DON'T BELONG IN THE VALLEY.
SHOULD WE FOLLOW THEM?
NOT TONIGHT. TONIGHT WE HAVE TO GO TO THE VILLAGE OF OAK BOTTOM AND STOP BALSAAD.

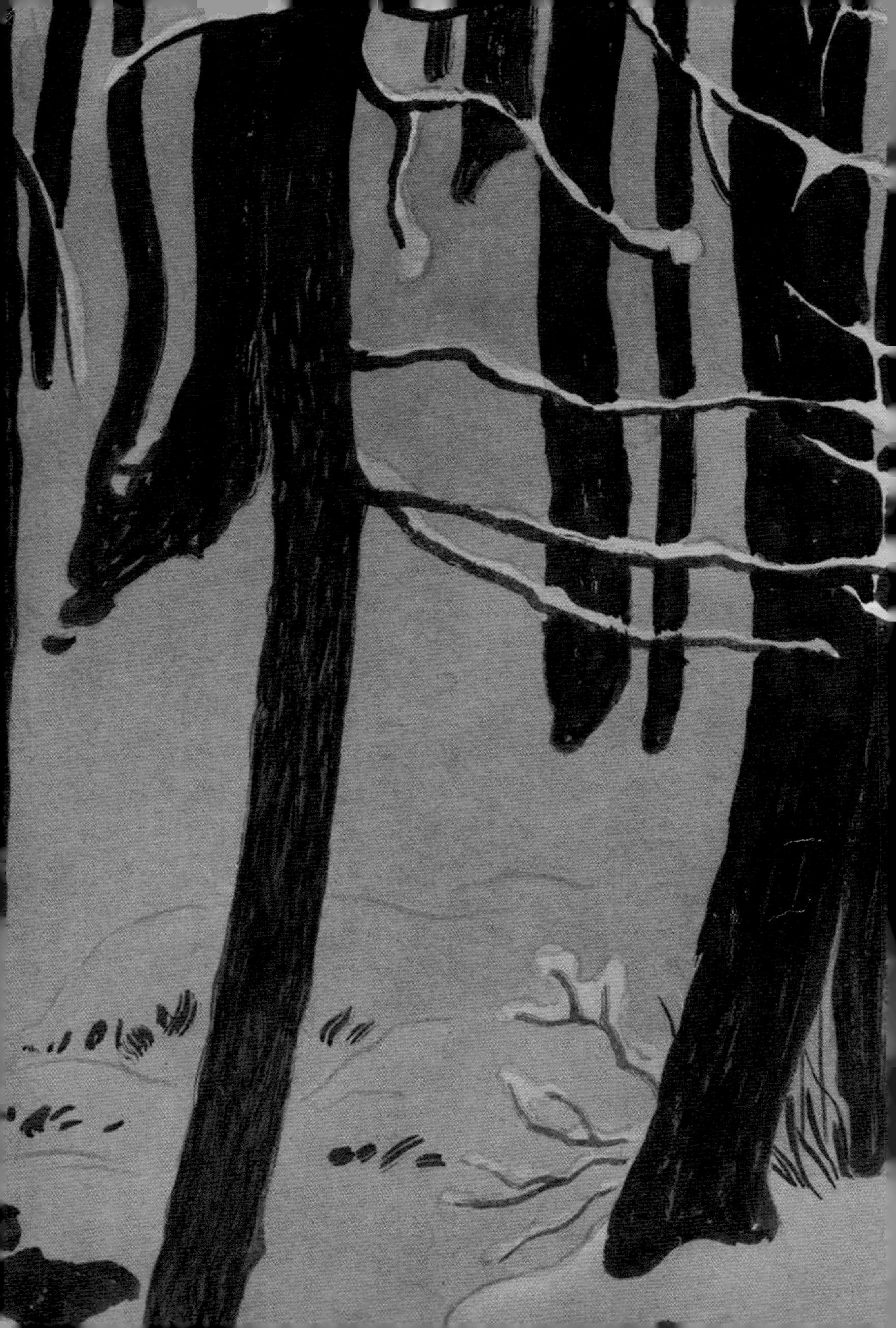

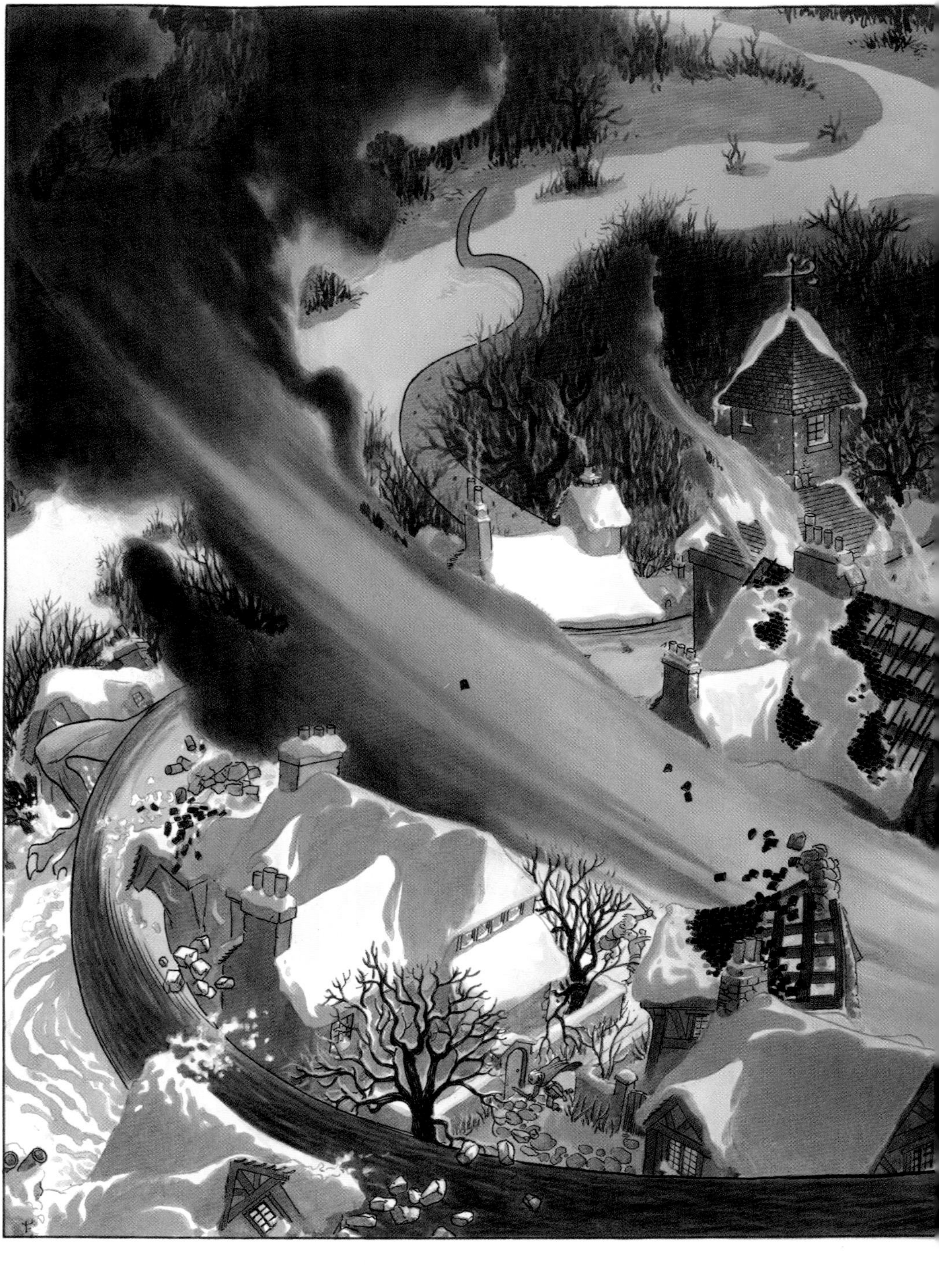

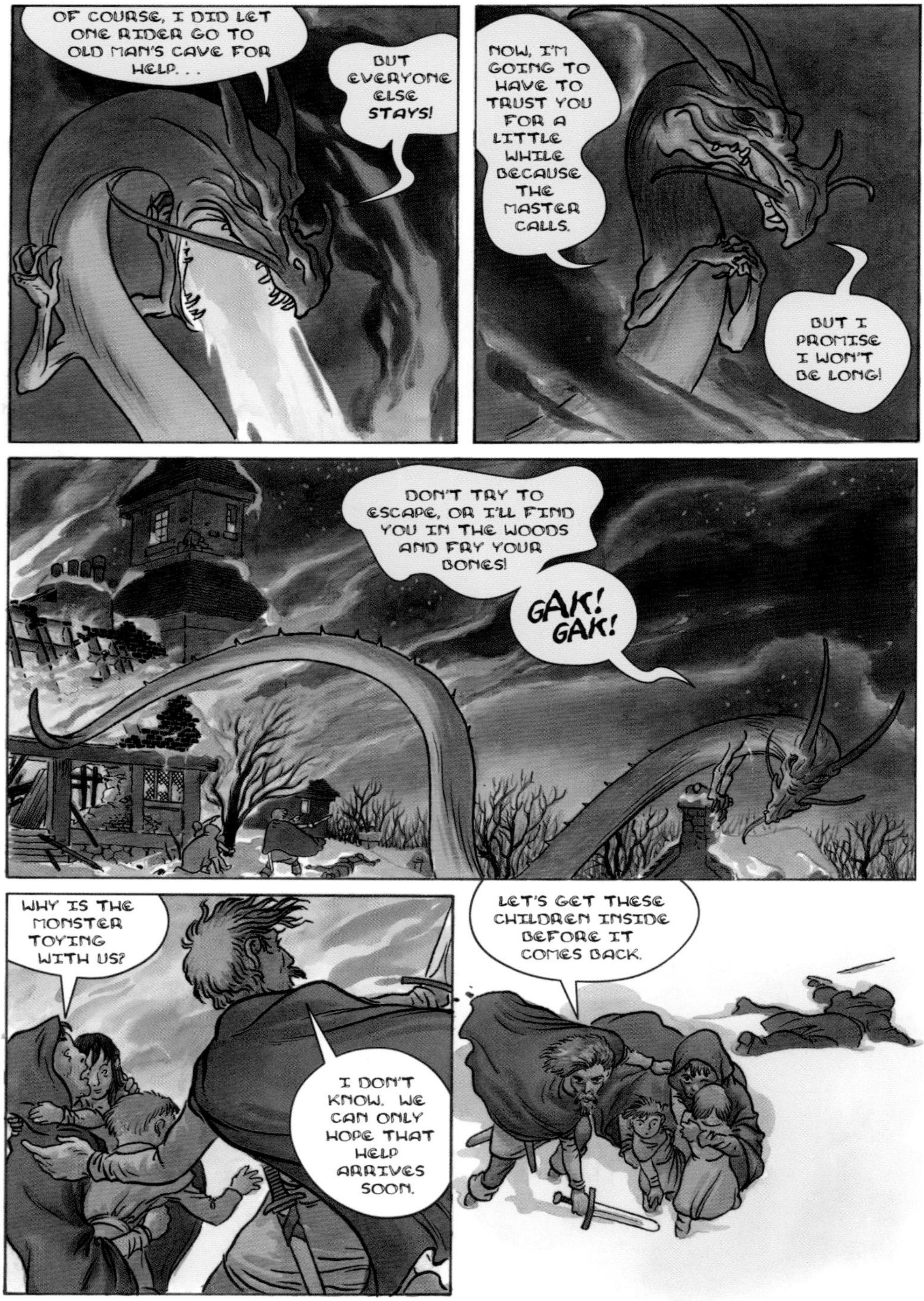
OF COURSE, I DID LET ONE RIDER GO TO OLD MAN'S CAVE FOR HELP. . .
BUT EVERYONE ELSE STAYS!
NOW, I'M GOING TO HAVE TO TRUST YOU FOR A LITTLE WHILE BECAUSE THE MASTER CALLS.
BUT I PROMISE I WON'T BE LONG!
DON'T TRY TO ESCAPE, OR I'LL FIND YOU IN THE WOODS AND FRY YOUR BONES!
GAK! GAK!
WHY IS THE MONSTER TOYING WITH US?
I DON'T KNOW. WE CAN ONLY HOPE THAT HELP ARRIVES SOON.
LET'S GET THESE CHILDREN INSIDE BEFORE IT COMES BACK.

THE PACT

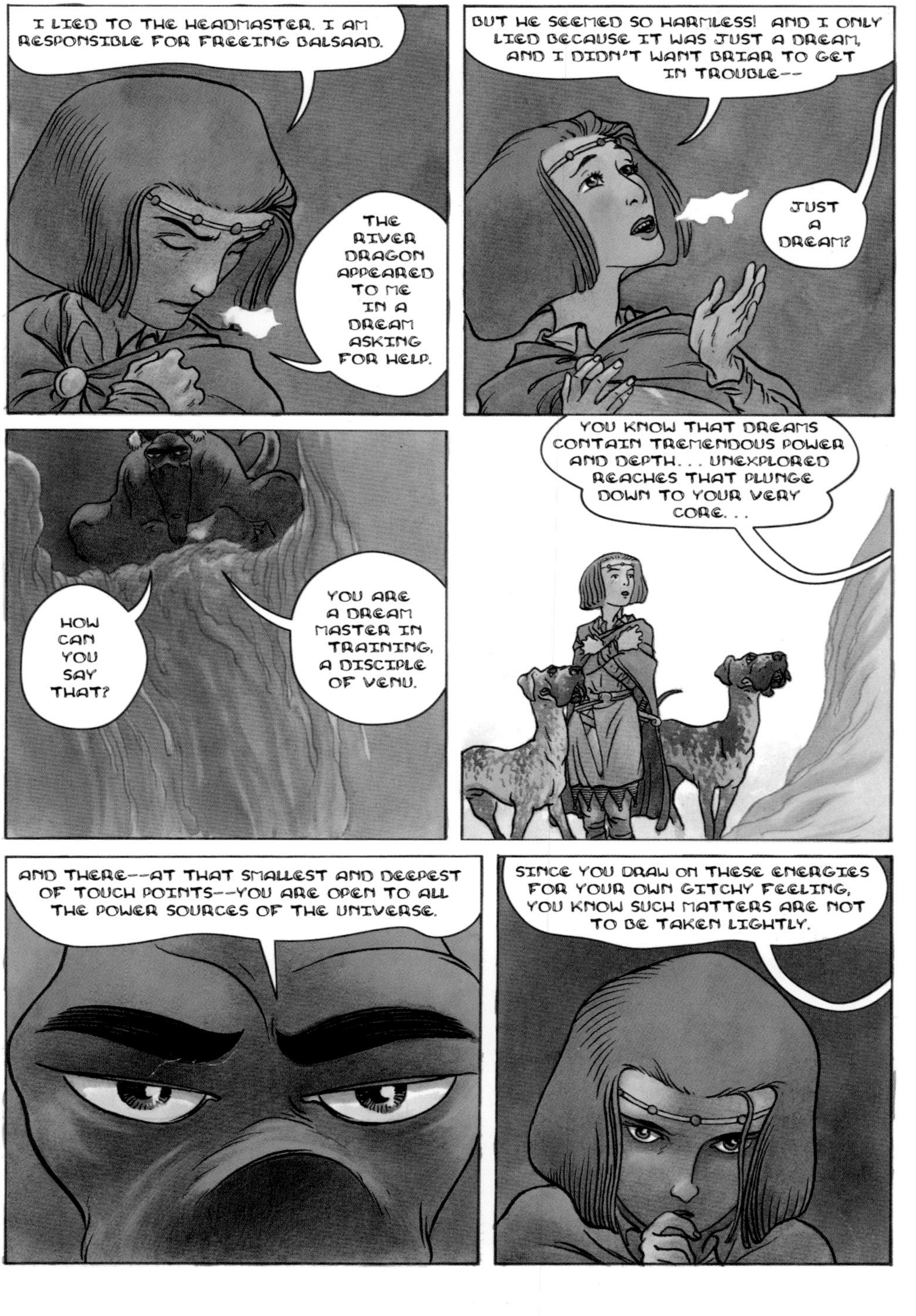
I LIED TO THE HEADMASTER. I AM RESPONSIBLE FOR FREEING BALSAAD.
THE RIVER DRAGON APPEARED TO ME IN A DREAM ASKING FOR HELP.
BUT HE SEEMED SO HARMLESS! AND I ONLY LIED BECAUSE IT WAS JUST A DREAM, AND I DIDN'T WANT BRIAR TO GET IN TROUBLE--
JUST A DREAM?
HOW CAN YOU SAY THAT?
YOU ARE A DREAM MASTER IN TRAINING, A DISCIPLE OF VENU.
YOU KNOW THAT DREAMS CONTAIN TREMENDOUS POWER AND DEPTH. . . UNEXPLORED REACHES THAT PLUNGE DOWN TO YOUR VERY CORE. . .
AND THERE--AT THAT SMALLEST AND DEEPEST OF TOUCH POINTS--YOU ARE OPEN TO ALL THE POWER SOURCES OF THE UNIVERSE.
SINCE YOU DRAW ON THESE ENERGIES FOR YOUR OWN GITCHY FEELING, YOU KNOW SUCH MATTERS ARE NOT TO BE TAKEN LIGHTLY.

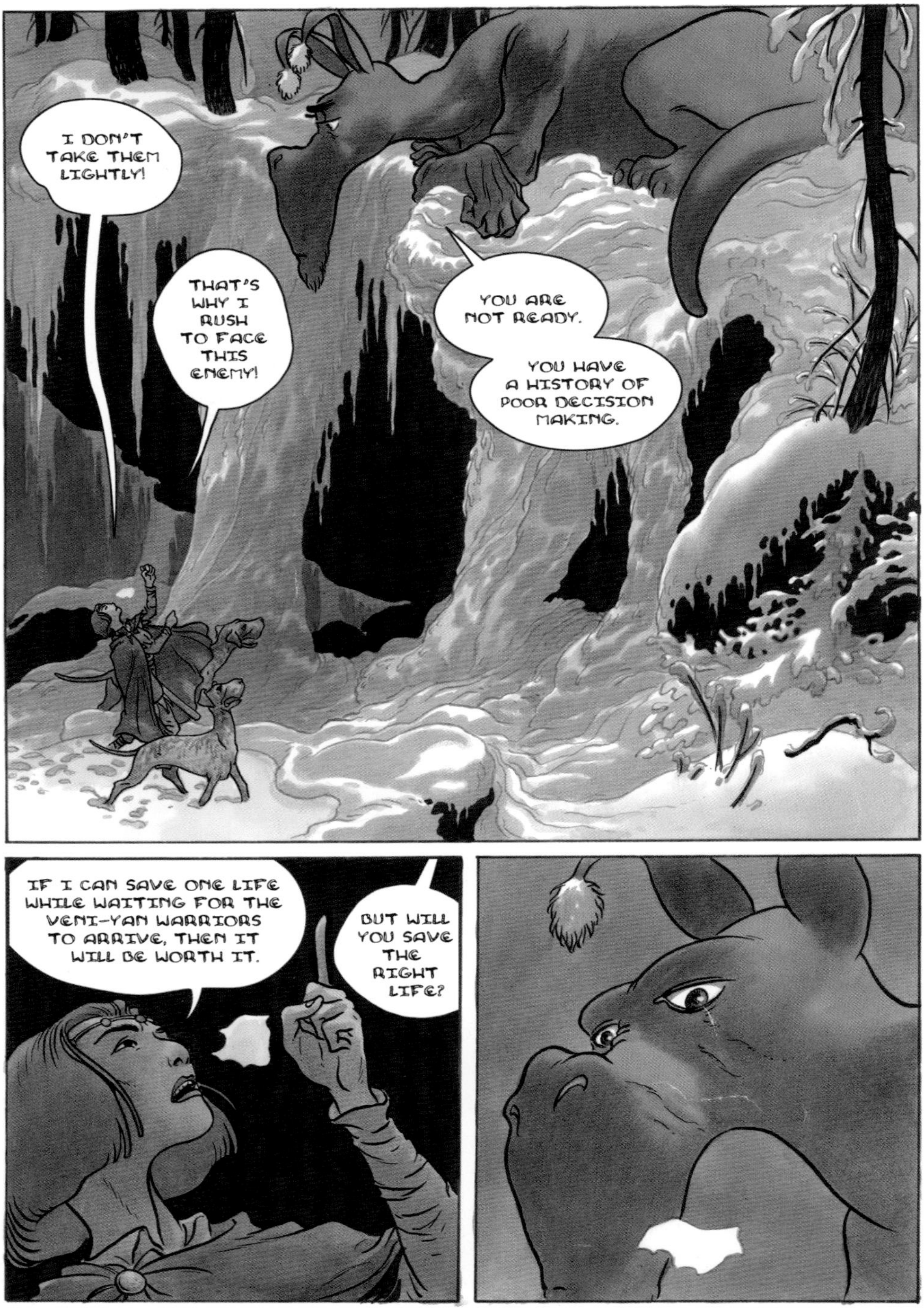
I DON'T TAKE THEM LIGHTLY!
THAT'S WHY I RUSH TO FACE THIS ENEMY!
YOU ARE NOT READY.
YOU HAVE A HISTORY OF POOR DECISION MAKING.
IF I CAN SAVE ONE LIFE WHILE WAITING FOR THE VENI-YAN WARRIORS TO ARRIVE, THEN IT WILL BE WORTH IT.
BUT WILL YOU SAVE THE RIGHT LIFE?

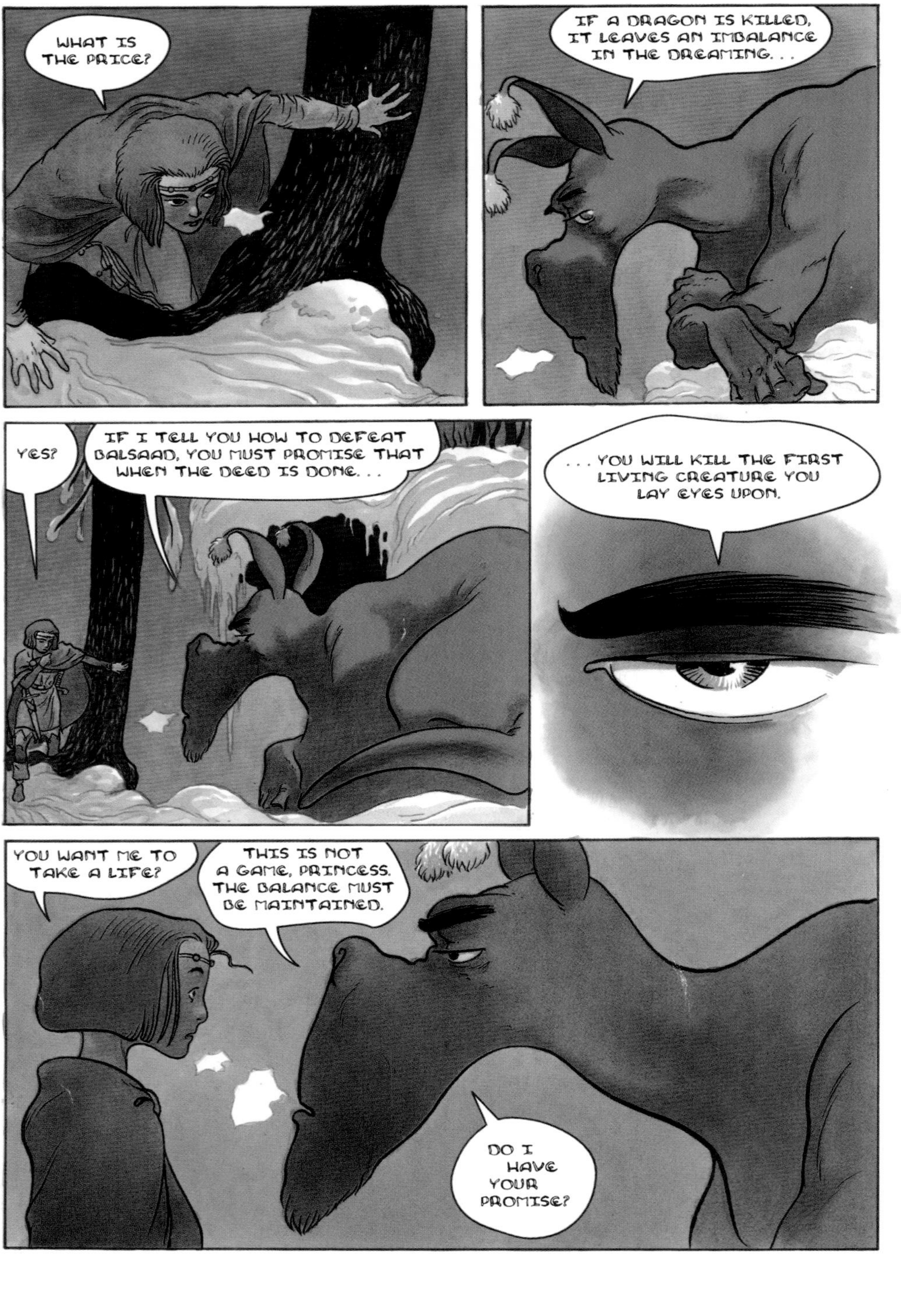
WHAT IS THE PRICE?
IF A DRAGON IS KILLED, IT LEAVES AN IMBALANCE IN THE DREAMING. . .
YES?
IF I TELL YOU HOW TO DEFEAT BALSAAD, YOU MUST PROMISE THAT WHEN THE DEED IS DONE. . .
. . . YOU WILL KILL THE FIRST LIVING CREATURE YOU LAY EYES UPON.
YOU WANT ME TO TAKE A LIFE?
THIS IS NOT A GAME, PRINCESS. THE BALANCE MUST BE MAINTAINED.
DO I HAVE YOUR PROMISE?

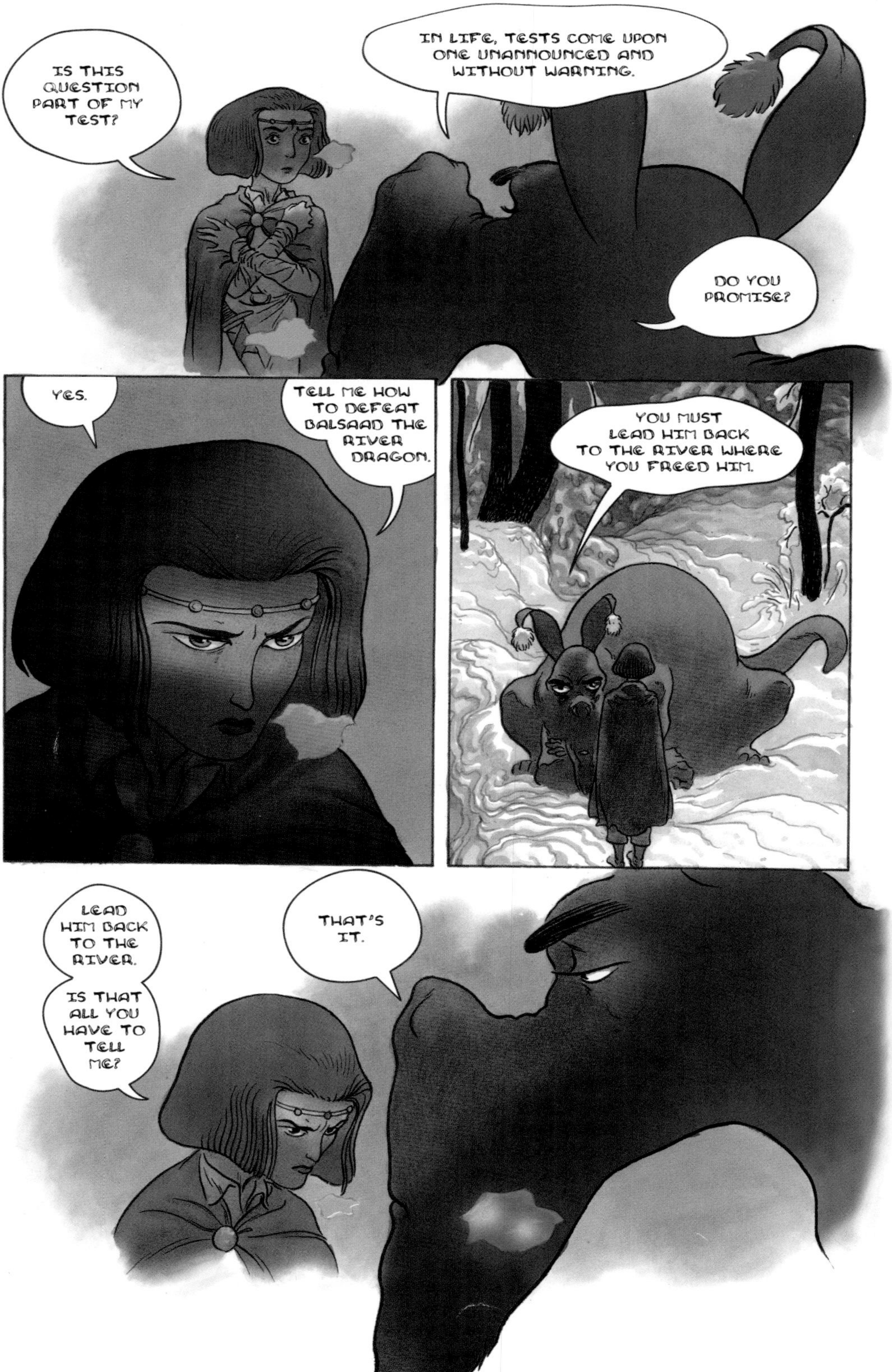
IS THIS QUESTION PART OF MY TEST?
IN LIFE, TESTS COME UPON ONE UNANNOUNCED AND WITHOUT WARNING.
DO YOU PROMISE?
YES.
TELL ME HOW TO DEFEAT BALSAAD THE RIVER DRAGON.
YOU MUST LEAD HIM BACK TO THE RIVER WHERE YOU FREED HIM.
LEAD HIM BACK TO THE RIVER.
IS THAT ALL YOU HAVE TO TELL ME?
THAT'S IT.

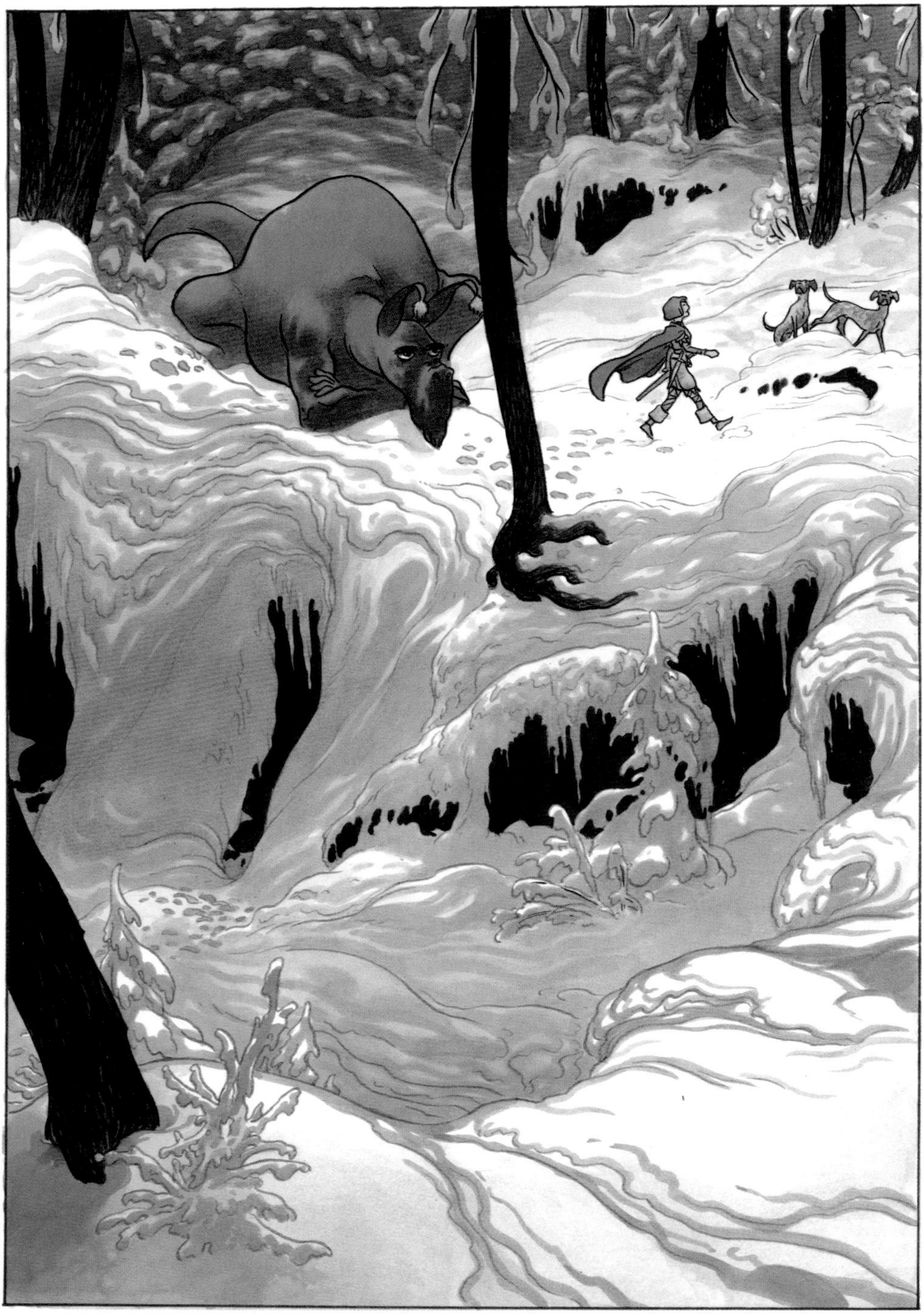

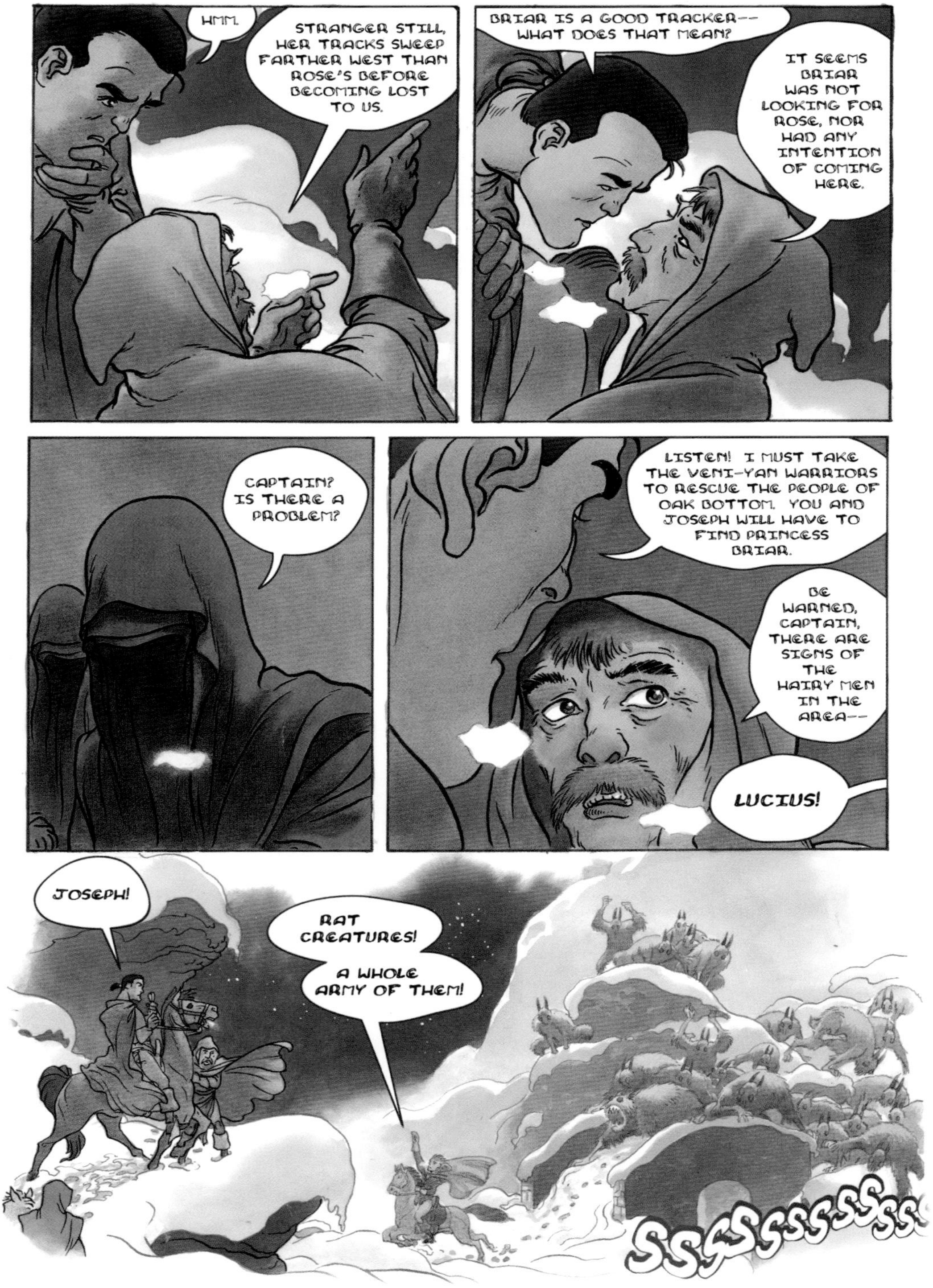
HMM.
STRANGER STILL, HER TRACKS SWEEP FARTHER WEST THAN ROSE'S BEFORE BECOMING LOST TO US.
BRIAR IS A GOOD TRACKER-- WHAT DOES THAT MEAN?
IT SEEMS BRIAR WAS NOT LOOKING FOR ROSE, NOR HAD ANY INTENTION OF COMING HERE.
CAPTAIN? IS THERE A PROBLEM?
LISTEN! I MUST TAKE THE VENI-YAN WARRIORS TO RESCUE THE PEOPLE OF OAK BOTTOM. YOU AND JOSEPH WILL HAVE TO FIND PRINCESS BRIAR.
BE WARNED, CAPTAIN, THERE ARE SIGNS OF THE HAIRY MEN IN THE AREA--
LUCIUS!
JOSEPH!
RAT CREATURES!
A WHOLE ARMY OF THEM!
SSSSSSSSSSSSS

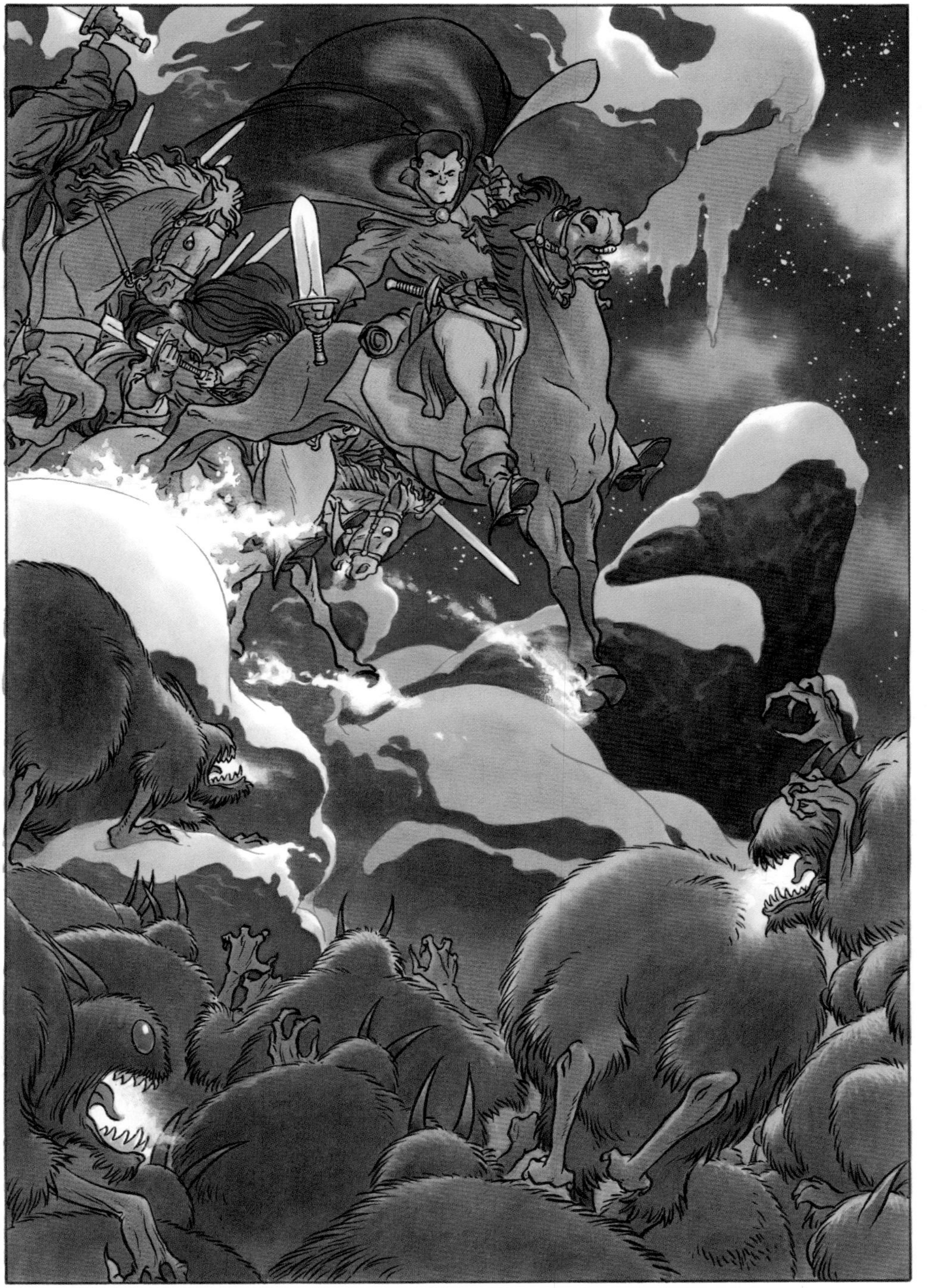

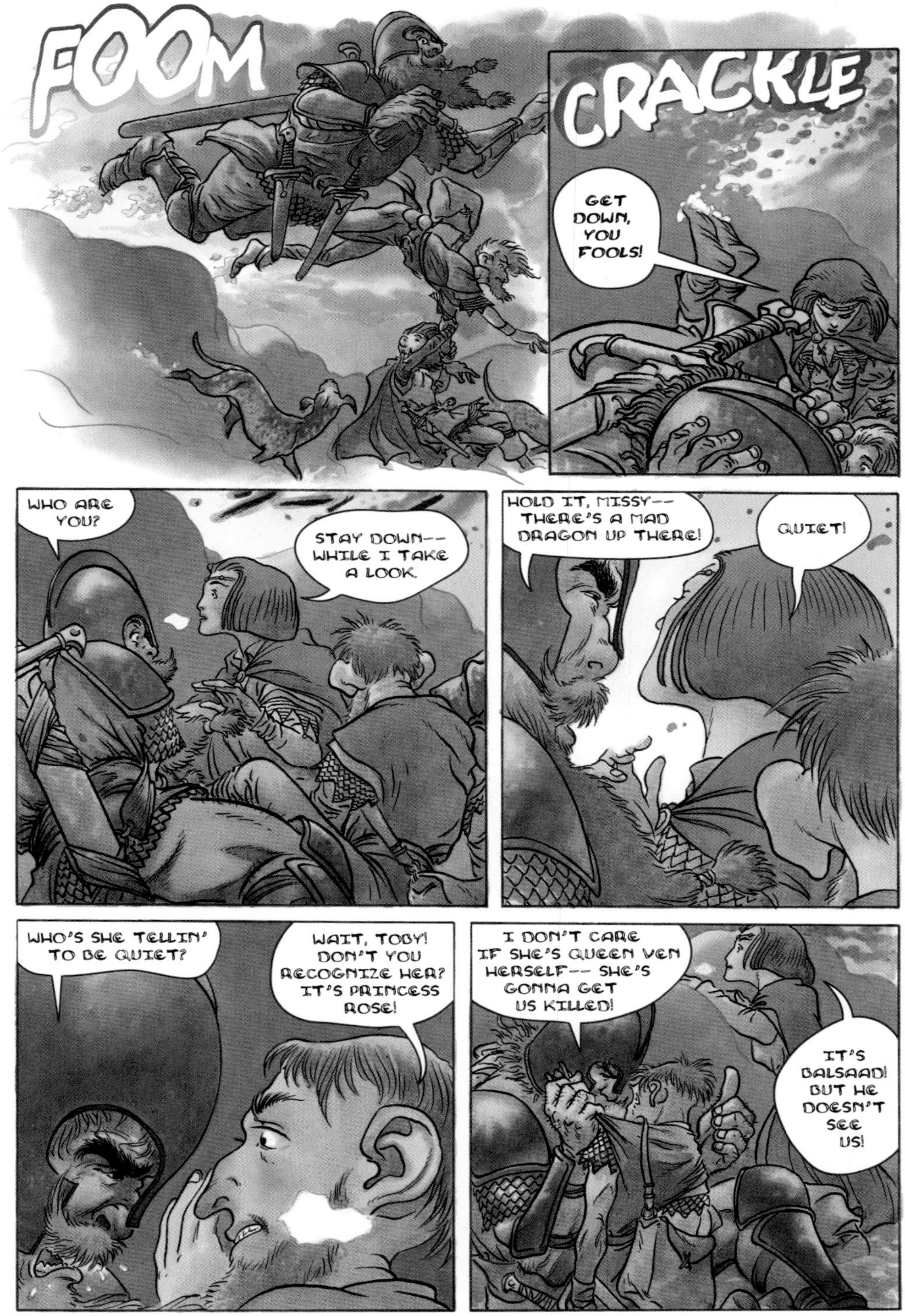
FOOM
CRACKLE
GET DOWN, YOU FOOLS!
WHO ARE YOU?
STAY DOWN-- WHILE I TAKE A LOOK.
HOLD IT, MISSY-- THERE'S A MAD DRAGON UP THERE!
QUIET!
WHO'S SHE TELLIN' TO BE QUIET?
WAIT, TOBY! DON'T YOU RECOGNIZE HER? IT'S PRINCESS ROSE!
I DON'T CARE IF SHE'S QUEEN VEN HERSELF-- SHE'S GONNA GET US KILLED!
IT'S BALSAAD! BUT HE DOESN'T SEE US!

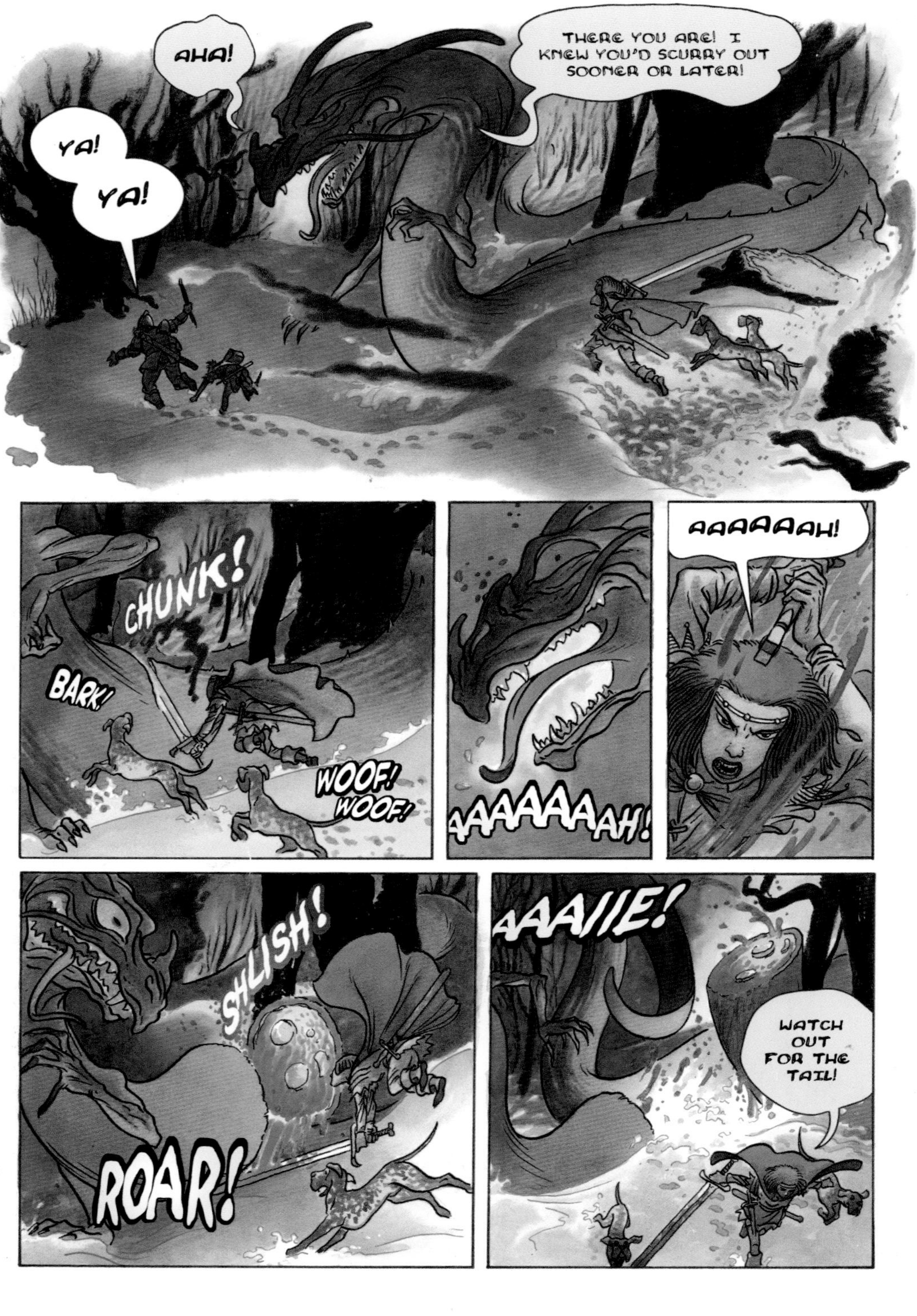
AHA!
THERE YOU ARE! I KNEW YOU'D SCURRY OUT SOONER OR LATER!
YA!
YA!
CHUNK!
BARK!
WOOF! WOOF!
AAAAAAAH!
AAAAAAH!
SHLISH!
ROAR!
AAAIIE!
WATCH OUT FOR THE TAIL!

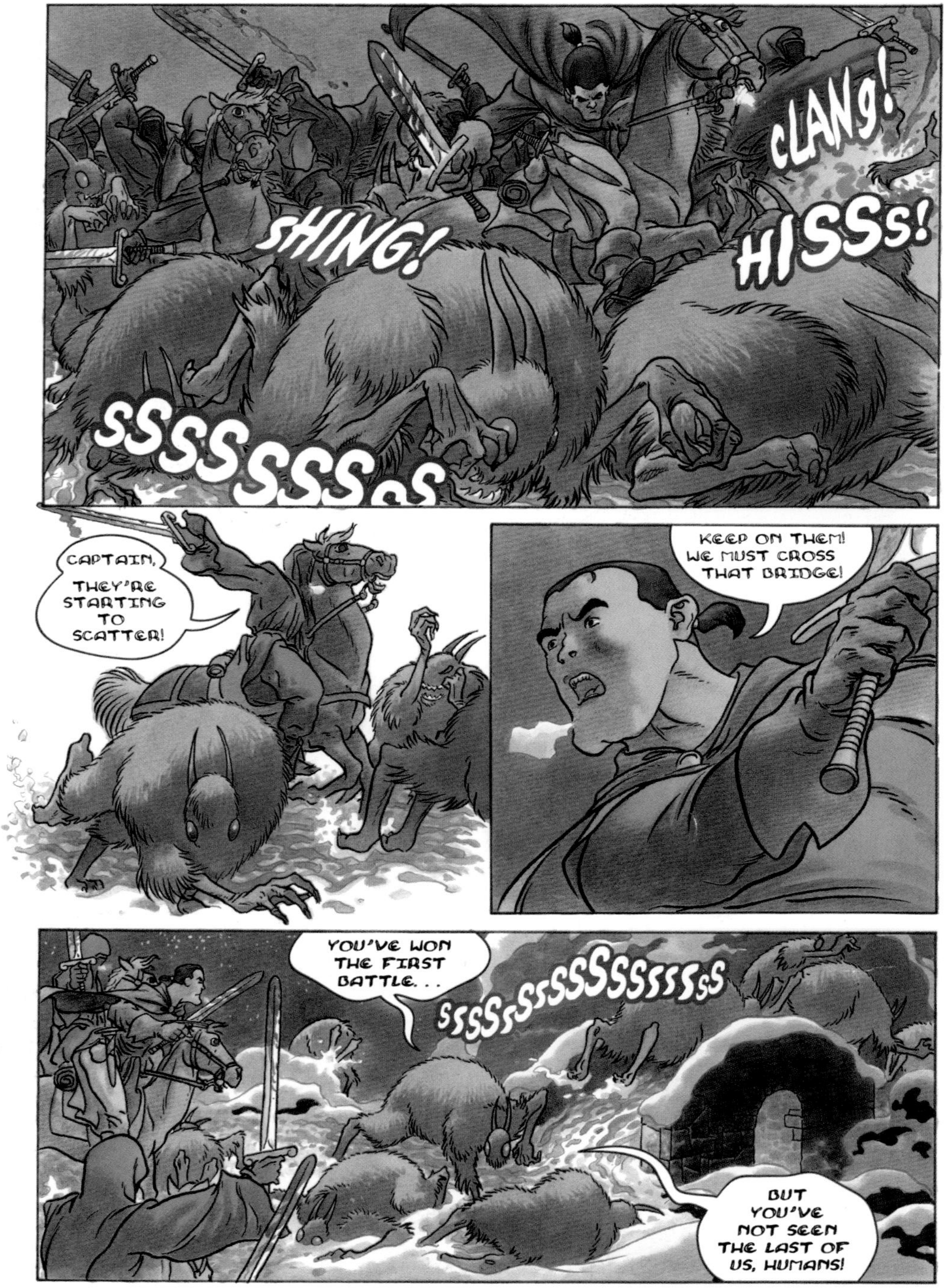
CLANG!
HISSs!
SHING!
SSSSSSSSSS
CAPTAIN, THEY'RE STARTING TO SCATTER!
KEEP ON THEM! WE MUST CROSS THAT BRIDGE!
YOU'VE WON THE FIRST BATTLE. . .
SSSSSSSSSSSSSSSSSS
BUT YOU'VE NOT SEEN THE LAST OF US, HUMANS!

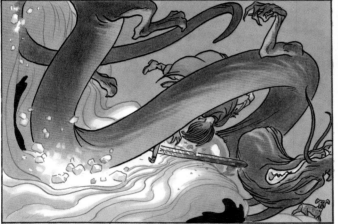

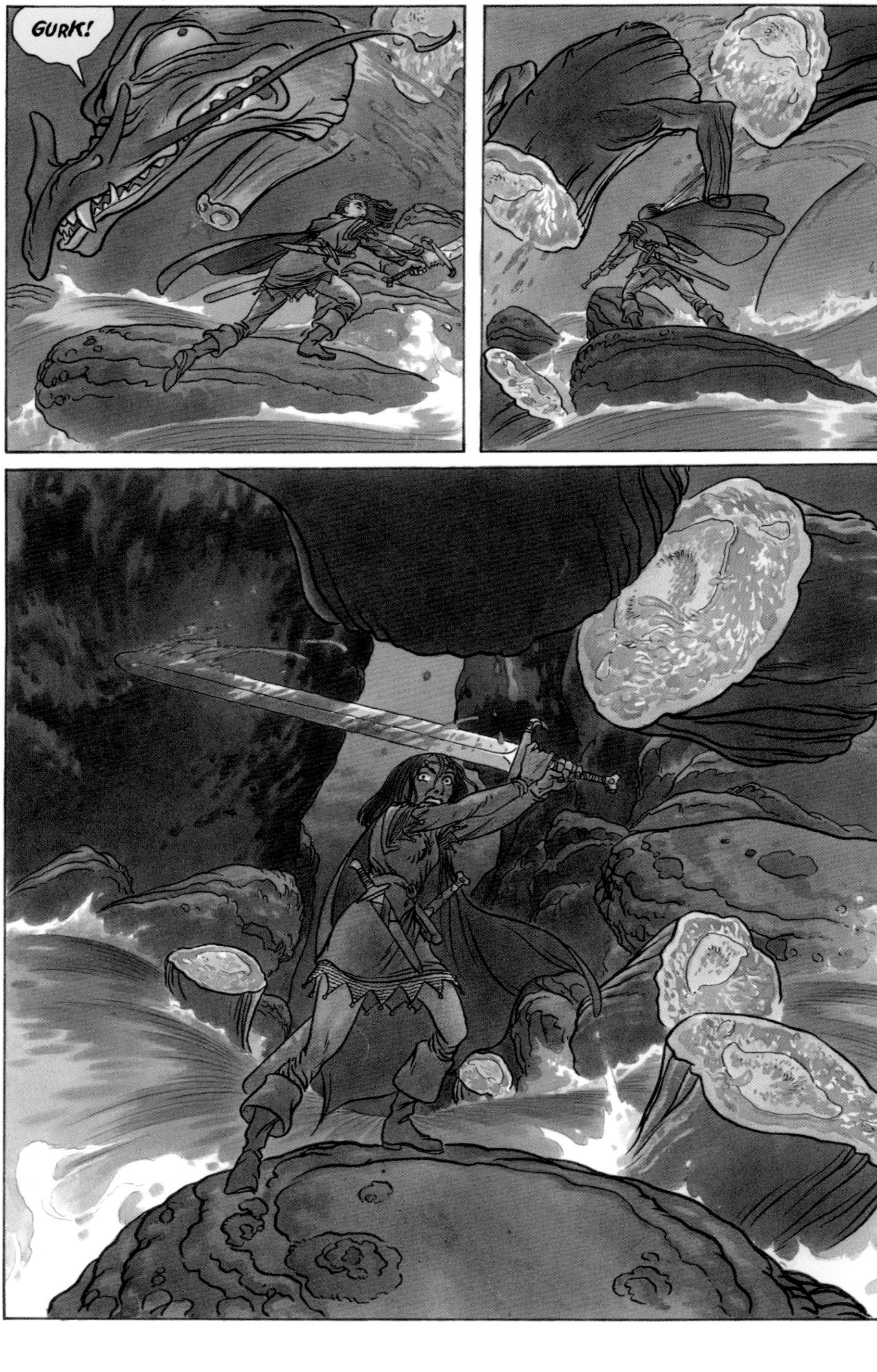
GURK!

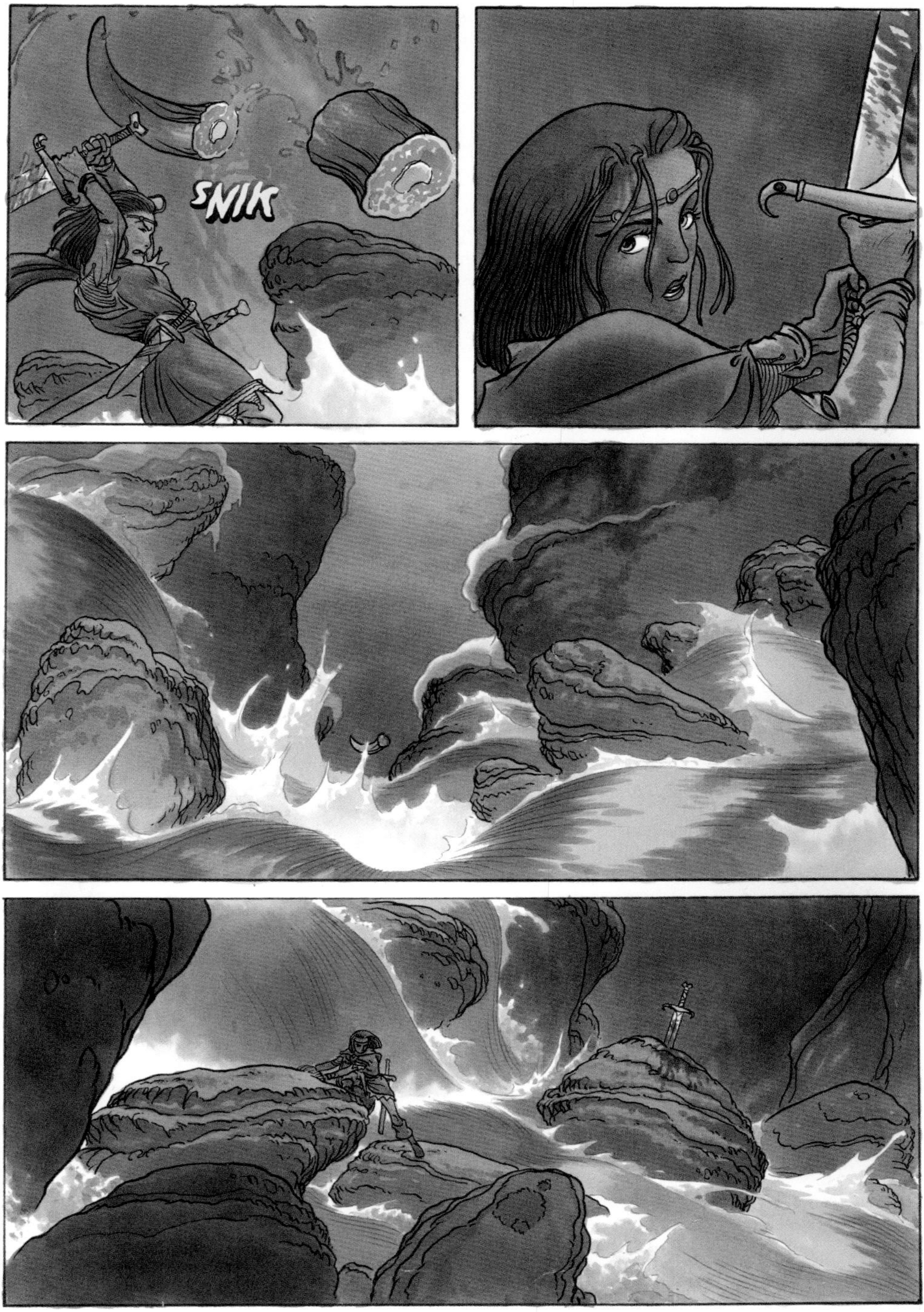
SNIK

HE TURNED ME INTO AN OLD CRONE TO PUNISH ME FOR MY FAILURE.

HELP ME, ROSE. I--

ROSE? WHY ARE YOU HOLDING THAT KNIFE?

I GAVE MY WORD TO THE GREAT RED DRAGON THAT I WOULD KILL THE FIRST LIVING CREATURE I SAW...

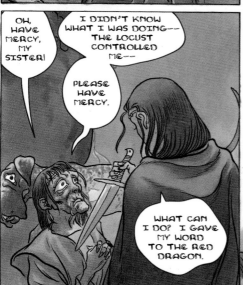

OH, HAVE MERCY, MY SISTER!

I DIDN'T KNOW WHAT I WAS DOING-- THE LOCUST CONTROLLED ME--

PLEASE HAVE MERCY.

WHAT CAN I DO? I GAVE MY WORD TO THE RED DRAGON.

KILL THE DOG INSTEAD. YOU SAW IT AT ALMOST THE SAME TIME-- THE DRAGON WON'T CARE IF YOU SUBSTITUTE AS LONG AS BALANCE IS MAINTAINED.

PLEASE, SISTER.

I'M YOUR OWN FLESH AND BLOOD.

I BEG YOU TO DO THE RIGHT THING.

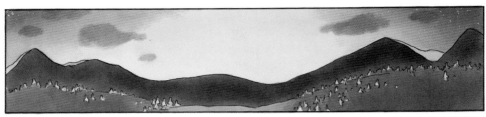

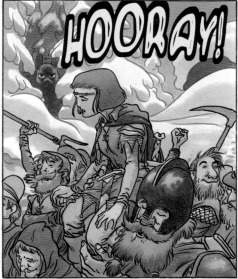

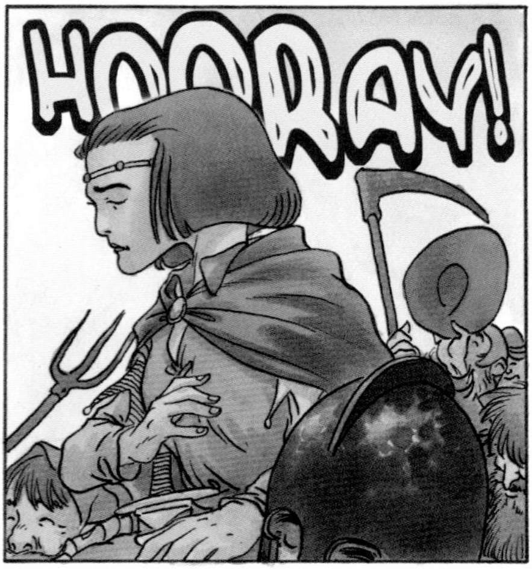
HOORAY!

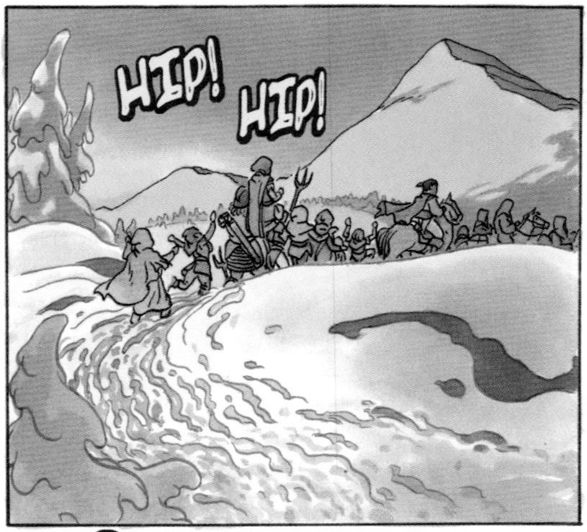
HIP!
HIP!

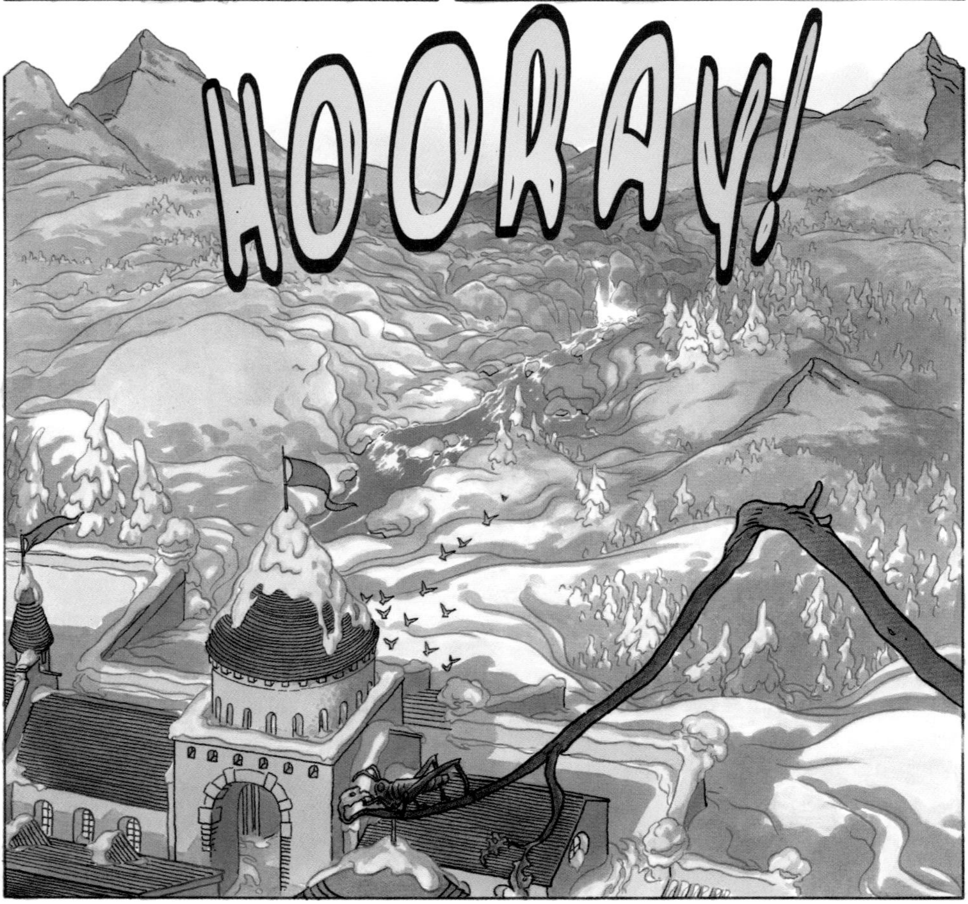
HOORAY!

THE END

About JEFF SMITH

JEFF SMITH was born and raised in the American Midwest and learned about cartooning from comic strips, comic books, and watching animated shorts on TV. After four years of drawing comic strips for The Ohio State University's student newspaper and co-founding Character Builders animation studio in 1986, Smith launched the comic book *BONE* in 1991. Between *BONE* and other comics projects, Smith spends much of his time on the international guest circuit promoting comics and the art of graphic novels. Visit him at www.boneville.com.

About CHARLES VESS

CHARLES VESS has published award-winning works with Marvel, DC, and Cartoon Books, and one of his two Eisner awards was for his paintings in *Rose*. Vess collaborated with Neil Gaiman on their book *Stardust* (now a movie on DVD), for which he won the World Fantasy Award for Best Artist in 1999. He also illustrated *Seven Wild Sisters*, written by Charles de Lint, and *The Green Man: Tales from the Mythic Forest*, both of which were American Library Association Best Books. The design and co-sculpting of a bronze fountain based on *A Midsummer Night's Dream* has kept him busy for the last two years. Vess lives on a small farm in Virginia, and you can visit him at www.greenmanpress.com.

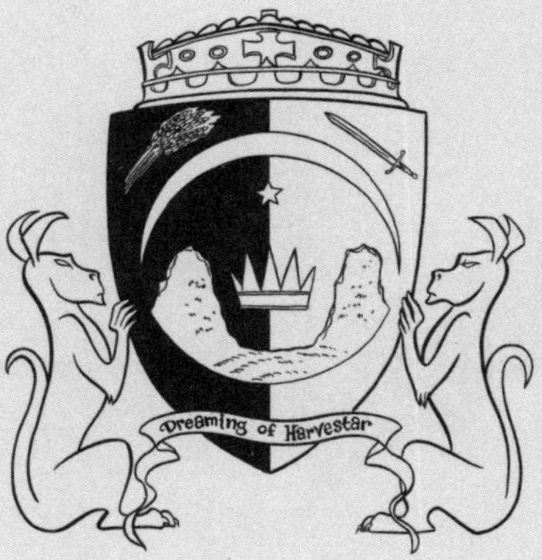
Dreaming of Harvestar

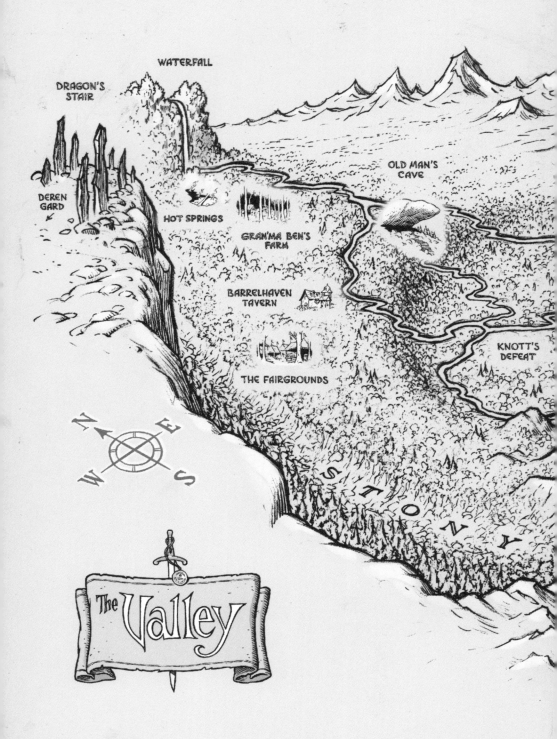

WATERFALL

DRAGON'S
STAIR

OLD MAN'S
CAVE

DEREN
GARD

HOT SPRINGS

GRAN'MA BEN'S
FARM

BARRELHAVEN
TAVERN

KNOTT'S
DEFEAT

THE FAIRGROUNDS

N
E
W
S

STONY

The Valley